running with the grunion:
stories of peace & aloha

tia ballantine

Copyright © 2016 Tia Ballantine
All Rights Reserved
ISBN-13: 978-0997803310 (Lelepono Press)
ISBN-10: 0997803312

ACKNOWLEDGMENTS

Many thanks to Betty Winstedt, Vicky Durand, and Gloria Jacobson for providing peaceful shelter and kind companionship during the months I wrote these stories and many more heartfelt thanks for listening so attentively as I read them aloud.

For all who work for Peace.

For those who have suffered PTSD
yet still see their fellow human beings
as intrinsically good and kind.

Life is short. Live lovingly. Do no harm.
Practice random acts of Kindness.
Occupy Your Mind: Think Responsibly.
Be generous. Make art.

Why not?

Preface:

These stories were written, day-by-day, over a period of months after I had emerged still breathing but profoundly shaken from an extraordinarily traumatic situation. I survived and was finally once again on safe ground, but then I discovered I was not so safe after all. My world was spinning.

After being startled awake, again and again, night after night, after have idyllic seashore scenes disappear behind vivid scenes of violence, raging fires, guns and more guns, folks with faces twisted into expressions of raw aggression, mouths gaping, hands punching air, I realized I was suffering from PTSD. But as I was not military and as I, like too many well-educated Americans, had no health insurance, I knew clearly I would have to find my own way past crashing grating waking dreams if I were to be once again happy, healthy and truly alive.

I decided I would negotiate my way through the shallows of brutal memory using the only tools for healing I had at my disposal. I would write my way through but with caution care and what I hoped was good will. I set myself certain parameters. I would *not* rant nor would I describe over and over again the particular events that had caused the PTSD. And I would stay away from affixing blame.

Instead, I would write stories with sympathetic characters who might have suffered some life-changing event but who found solution through art, living, and perhaps silence. I would try to describe matters of the heart as mitigated by the mind, matters of the mind expanded by the heart.

Within the stories I would attempt to unwrap those difficult societal problems created by unconscious attitudes that surface through equally unconscious behavior – racism, sexism, ageism, prejudice against those who live near the borders of society . . . performers, artists, free-thinkers. But, I told myself, if ever I found myself veering into barren landscape of the didactic or the sentimental, I would stop. Start again.

I wanted my stories to move the heart and engage the mind, invite readers to consider the oppressions imposed upon all of us by war and religion, but as a writer, I didn't want to come off as some stern-faced moralist wagging my finger under the reader's nose. I wanted the stories to effervesce as much with humor as with compassion. I didn't want just *my* voice to be heard. I wanted the voices of my characters to be heard, the voice of the other. Many of these stories are written in the first person but, of course, that first person is not me. I wanted a lot, I guess . . . but don't we all? As I wrote, I knew that *mostly* all I wanted was to return to the world of wonder, light and joy. I wanted the demons gone. I wanted my life back.

Did my plan work? Did I banish the PTSD?

I can only claim that the solution was partial. There are some things loving human beings are incapable of banishing from memory and those things remain as terrors attached to bone. I might never be able to eradicate completely the most persistent nagging reminders of human meanness. Nonetheless, I can say that writing the stories served me well. I don't think I would be functioning as clearly as kindly as generously today if I had simply retreated into the anger and pain produced by those disastrous months that left me suffering PTSD.

I wrote dozens and dozens of stories, twenty of which I saved. These I offer you. I enjoyed writing these tales, and I hope you enjoy reading them. Perhaps you will find them as necessary as I did. If not, I hope you find them at least somewhat entertaining or curious or both.

These are *stories*, 100% fictional. All characters are fictional. Any resemblance to real people or real events is entirely coincidental.

* * *

contents

An Introduction: *The Family Sacrifice*	1
Tinker Tailor Soldier Sailor	11
Running with the Grunion	21
Harmonics	29
Transplanting Family Trees	37
Rivers	45
Learning to Fly	53
Cloudbreak	61
Regreso	69
Whistlestop	79

January Tides	87
Space Between	95
Slow River	103
Kali has no clothes	113
Wardrobe	119
Borderline	127
Dear Killer Boy	135
Low Tide	143
Victory Gardens	149
Coda	155

An Introduction: The Family Sacrifice

The stories of our lives are skewed by memory, either our own or that of others, but those twists and turns provide us with an emotional truth that grants us the patience to listen attentively to the unruly conversations of our own heart and mind and to those wander about in the environments where we live and grow. I am interested in stories of origin, myths about the origin of the world, but also in the simpler stories of human birth. I think that the circumstances of birth may describe something of the person, not an astrological truth revealed by the more profound movements of the planets, but something innately human and somehow true, and so before I dive in and tell you other stories, fictional tales pulled from my heart, I would like to first tell you the story of my birth as it has been told to me and as I have recovered it through artifacts of memory and photography. Then, I will offer you the perhaps more fantastical yet equally tender stories written while I was living alone on the beach in Makaha after returning from treacherous months that left me gasping. That's another story. The poet Muriel Rukeyser once noted that, "The world is made up, not of atoms, but of stories!" Stories are how we build our world. Let's start building! Here, then, is the story of how I became "the family sacrifice."

I was born at the height of summer but for most of my life, I have celebrated my birthday in the dead of winter, a little fact that once earned me ten dollars from Scholastic Magazine as payment for that "mind-boggling" scientific riddle, "mind-boggling," of course, only to those who are more comfortable with the simple organization of time as that which affects the world that swells and shrinks about them – their house, their town, their state, and maybe their country, but there must be whole cotillions of those people at home in such comfort zones because Scholastic snapped up my riddle and printed it. The solution to the riddle is not really that difficult. Someone living in the northern hemisphere but born in the southern hemisphere is born in the summer but celebrates her birthday in the winter. It's that simple, but what makes my birth interesting is how and why I was born in the high mountains of Peru to parents who were not military and who were not wealthy. That . . . and what happened in the brief period between my birth and the more widely celebrated birth of a baby who grew up to lay the foundation for churches and steeples everywhere.

My parents were artists, performers and writers. My father was an accomplished illustrator and a writer who published more than ten books during his lifetime, writing about circus, animals, the land, travel, and music. He wrote life, and illustrated his compassionate and insightful stories with his equally perceptive and distinctive pen and ink drawings. He was also a serious clown with a sly sense of humor and a keen intelligence, a humanist with a deeply abiding social conscience who later became the first dean of the Clown College in Florida. After graduating from Pomona College, my mother abandoned her native California and headed for NYC and the stage. Before my birth, she worked first as a comedienne, performing as a "straight woman" in a comedic vaudeville act, then as a showgirl, one of Billy Rose's "long stem roses," and finally as the Snow Queen of Ringling Brothers, Barnum and Bailey Circus, riding in a gilded carriage drawn by six high-stepping white horses with long combed manes that flamed from side to side as the horses tossed their heads and whinnied as might wild horses just put to halter. Balancing easily in six-inch heels and dressed in a form-fitting silver-spangled outfit that included a headdress topped with three-foot ostrich plumes, my six-foot tall mother stood statuesque, holding the reins of the spirited horses, with her King (the diminutive Prince Paul) by her side, his head well below her waist, bowing and waving as the carriage rolled along the sawdust track on the outer edge of the circus rings.

My father made the same circuit, but he was on foot, walking determinedly, as a sailor carrying a mermaid. From his head down to his waist, he was pure mermaid with matted red curls, wearing a prominent mermaid bra fashioned of wooden white-painted pearls. His white-gloved hands were decorated with oversize rings set with glass stones that sparked and danced as he gestured seductively to the crowd. From his waist down, he was sailor, dressed in Navy issue white cotton ducks and oversized clown shoes that flapped loudly as he tromped about the ring. Made of papier-maché, the sailor's torso was attached to my father's back, the sailor's head with his loopy painted smile thrown back, long sailor arms grasping the mermaid's svelte waist. The mermaid's tail, also brightly painted papier-maché, floated to the front from the sailor's crotch. It was a brilliant costume, gently commenting on what it is to live between myth and reality, knowing both male and female in one body. Walking stalwartly about the ring, blowing kisses with his mermaid hand, he was man-woman, real and mythological, with neither male nor female privileged. His act drew catcalls and laughter from the crowd but deep admiration from my mother. As a Phi Beta Kappa graduate in English literature, she read the back-story and understood that philosophical statement he was communicating went far beyond just another clever costume. She wanted to know the man who had conceived such a brilliantly simple walk-around act, capable of simultaneously eliciting guffaws, compassion, and something that came dangerously close to grace.

When she finally met him, she learned that he was also a talented illustrator and writer who had joined the show because circus was primary in his life and also because he was writing and illustrating a story for Life magazine about circus and the life of a clown. It was not long before she was a part of that life. After the season ended, they were married at her mother's home is San Bernardino, California. It was not a traditional wedding but there was a three-tiered cake complete with tiny figurines of the bride and groom standing hand-in-hand on the white snow of the cake. The figurine of the bride was a perfect replica of my mother as the Snow Queen and the groom was my father, dressed not in his mermaid costume but in another more sober Beckettesque overcoat complete with voluminous pockets good for holding all kinds of magic, I'm sure. His face, painted with his signature clown makeup, was looking up adoringly at my mother and hers was tilted down towards him.

I never knew what happened to these figurines. Perhaps they were fashioned of marzipan and my mother ate one and my father the other. I only saw these tiny images of love in the meticulous and tender drawing my father made of the lively celebration following the ceremony, including a self-portrait himself as he lifted Prince Paul to kiss the bride and a bold portrait of my talented grandmother, a talented portrait painter, positioned in the foreground of the teeming crowd, one eye hidden by her wide-brimmed hat.

My older brother was born exactly nine-months after the wedding, my sister a year and some months later, but when my mother found herself pregnant again the following year, she put her foot down. No more babies would be born in winter. She gathered up her babies and flew off to California, but by the time my father had located what he thought might be the perfect location for the birth of the new member of the Ballantine tribe and by the time my mother had convinced her mother to come along on the grand adventure, by that time, my mother was very nearly eight months pregnant. No matter. Never one to stay put, she gathered up her babies again and took off with her mother on a puddle jumper, a plane that set down every five hundred miles or so as it spit its way across the country, headed for Miami where my father waited expectantly.

It is certainly pleasant in Miami in December, but Miami had not been selected as the ideal locale for the birth of the new baby. Soon, the entire little tribe traipsed off to the airport once again and climbed on yet another plane – this one bound for Lima, Peru. Lima, however, was judged a bit too hot and steamy for a December birth and so the trek continued. This time, babies and luggage were loaded on an inland train, headed for the mountains and Arequipa, where the midsummer temperatures would be a bit more bearable and where my father had secured three pleasant rooms in a pensione owned by Tia Bates. Each room had windows facing a distant view of Mount Misti and doors opening onto a lush inner courtyard overrun with bougainvillea and other surprising flowers tucked into this corner or that.

One of the older cities in Peru, founded in 1579, Arequipa sits in the shadow of three towering volcanoes, Mount Misti, Pichupichu, and Chachani. During the last few decades of the twentieth century, the city was the headquarters of the Shining Path Guerillas who struggled to wrest the reins for Peru's political future from the grasping hands of Belaunde and his fascist brethren, but at the time of my birth, Arequipa was a sleepy city of buildings built of chiseled chunks of pale almost white stone that glowed eerily in the moonlight and seemed to be impossibly white by day. To my mother, the thin air and the brilliant light were the magic she needed for a December birth.

The minute the family arrived at Tia Bates' boarding house, my father was off to explore the city, to check out the hospital and find (hopefully) a doctor who might tend to my mother and oversee my birth. The hospital was not hard to find – it was only a few blocks from the pensione – and before long my father located a doctor with a name that seemed to predict good fortune. Dr. Barrionuevo, whose name meant New City in English (New City was the site of our NY home), was surprised when my father asked to inspect the hospital. But why, sir, he asked, why do you need a hospital? Is not your wife about to give birth? Surely, he said, I can come to the pensione. Would she not be more comfortable there?

My father had thought this a strange and backward notion, and my mother (and her mother too) insisted that the birth would take place in the hospital. Poor Dr Barrionuevo tried valiantly to explain that the hospital was not the place for newborn babies, that the hospital was for the sick, the dying, the clinically infirm, but the more he explained the more my mother insisted. Finally he threw up his hands and asked that a room be cleaned and prepared for the *Americana, la loca,* who would soon arrive to give birth. And that is how I came to be born in El Hospital Goyaneche on the outskirts of Arequipa where daily a small herd of sheep wandered carelessly through an open door on one side of the main hall and crossed to another open door on the other side, moving as they had always moved from one pasture to the next.

As the hospital was designed for final days and had no ways or means to save lives, it was indeed fortunate that my birth was uncomplicated even quite serene. I was a large baby – 4.22 kg, nearly 9 lbs – but my mother was a large woman, standing just a shade over six feet tall in her stocking feet and this was her third birth. When shortly after midnight, I came screaming into the world, Nurse Laura took one look at my chunky limbs, my thick black hair and my purple blue skin and exclaimed, "Una pequeña Peruana, una Arequipeña!" She was convinced I was native born. She glanced approvingly at my father's pale blue eyes and silken blond hair and shook her finger at my mother. Many assumed that Laura could not see the world too clearly with her one good eye (the other was covered with a pirate patch), but she was right, of course, I did have black hair at birth and my skin was indeed covered with the hick purple slime of birth. Of course, my purple skin soon washed off and within weeks my thick black hair fell out, leaving behind a thin bit of fizzy almost white blond.

The morning after I entered the world with my eyes scrunched tight and my mouth pursed into a surprised 'O,' my brother and sister came to visit, stared for a brief moment at the strange purple baby before settling down to a grand game of chasing the sluggish lizards that slid down from the windowsills. Both lizard and toddlers hoped to find a stray beetle or two scurrying across the floor. My grandmother took one look at the room with its listing wrought iron bed and the scurrying wildlife lit by one swaying bare light bulb suspended from the ceiling and insisted most politely that mother return to the pensione where at least the maid came once a day to clean. At first, my mother was perfectly content to lay in her bed, puzzling her way through the local news, listening to the children laugh when the sheep went clattering across the hall down the way, but after her second meal of watery coffee and thin gruel, she agreed with mother that she would find better rest with Tia Bates.

Together they gathered the newspapers, the children, and the wilting roses my father had bought at some expense from a flower vendor near the cemetery and went back to pensione where full dinners, complete with fresh baked rolls, purple potatoes, and narrow crystal decanters of sherry, appeared every night at six thirty in the spacious airy dining room filled with tables set with silver and decorated with sprays of bougainvillea. That dining room with its wide windows looking out to Mount Misti would be the scene of the incident that earned me the nickname of the "Family Sacrifice" before I had the chance to take one step forward, before I could utter one word -- one cry -- in my defense.

To be born in mid-December is to be born into the middle of the Christmas frenzy, and to be born at that time in a Catholic country intensifies that frenzy. Every day, indeed very nearly every hour, in Arequipa, church bells solemnly rang announcing this mass or that service in honor of the Christ child, and every day but certainly not every hour, Tia Bates announced a new special dish to celebrate the day before the day after the day before the day close to the day the only day the special day, the birthday of the blessed one. Any day close to that birthday was a day worth celebrating, and "close to" was a phrase having many interpretations. Finally when the days counting down to the great day had grown so few that they might be counted on one hand, Tia Bates announced that this night's dinner would very special indeed and all guests should come dressed in their finest.

And what a dinner it was. First there were delicate salads of carved root vegetables carefully arranged on beds of greens carried on the same truck from Lima that had brought the fresh crab and sea scallops. Then, lamb chops, fresh peas, bright yellow sweet potatoes, warm delicate rolls wrapped in white linen, and tiny blue-glazed plates stacked with moons of butter. Just when everyone thought they could eat no more, Tia Bates announced that there would be coffee and cake. New candles, long white tapers, were brought to each table to replace those that had burned to stubs during the feast, and then she emerged from the kitchen with a wide tray filled with identical individual cakes for each table.

Each cake was slightly smaller than a newborn baby but obviously meant to resemble a baby tightly swaddled in silken purple cloths. Here is Peru, folks took seriously the dictum "Eat of my Body, Drink of my blood." This was the Christ child in effigy, meant to be consumed by finger-licking diners with worship in their hearts. Every baby cake lay on a silver platter surrounded by pink sugar roses, and every baby had a tiny baby face with rounded cheeks, staring eyes, and a delicate smile. Each face was identical, a pre-formed mask tucked beneath the folds of the smooth glazed icing.

My Episcopalian grandmother watched in horror as my mother pried the little mask of a face from the baby cake, revealing the moist yellow cake below. My mother then cut into the baby's head and offered the first piece to her mother. Speechless, my grandmother waved her dismay, refused the cake that was then handed to my father. My brother ate a bit of the baby's chest. My sister happily gobbled down the belly. I slept peacefully in my bassinet, wrapped in my brand-new purple dyed woolen blanket that my grandmother had bought from a vendor outside the cathedral. I'm sure I was quite unaware that the babycake was being devoured only inches away. I never had any nightmares of being eaten, but later my grandmother found purple icing matted on my cheek. Perhaps my brother or sister had offered me, the breathing purple baby, a bit of babycake.

Many years later, after my sons had grown and moved away, I found the little face mask from the babycake at my mother's house, lying on a bookshelf near the feet of a large ceramic elephant, glazed blue and gold. I asked my mother if I might have that little face with its rounded forehead, sly smile and still deeply etched eyes, and she agreed that the time had come for me to care for this precious mask. I have no idea what the mask is made of. It is not plastic, glass, metal or ceramic and it cannot be bread dough or bee pollen. In all these years, no insects have nibbled it, and it remains undamaged by water, heat or cold.

I still have that mask, stored in a wooden box together with a fading black and white photograph of our family, obviously taken in a local photography studio in Arequipa perhaps the same week as the feast of the babycake. Our family sits before a painted backdrop of Mount Misti, my mother seated with a bundle of baby in her arms, my father standing next to her, holding my sister in his arms. My brother stands in front of my mother, his small hands clutching the edge of her beautifully embroidered *huipil*. On the back of the photograph, someone had scrawled, *"The Family Sacrifice," her first week on earth*. The handwriting looks suspiciously like my own.

running with the grunion: *stories*

Tinker Tailor Soldier Sailor

At midnight, Ruth stepped onto the lawn. Walking across the wet grass towards the gate, she watched the moon dance across the waves beyond the lawn's edge. Impulsively, she clapped her hands, turned three times, made a wish, and then threw her head back to let the moon bathe her face. She hadn't done that for years. When she looked up, she gasped.

Stretched from the back of the valley all the way to far horizon of the sea was a narrow band of clouds, rippled like a salmon belly, swollen in its middle but gathered to a fine point at either end. Perfectly centered in the midsection of the lacework clouds was the full moon, lighting as pink gold the fish scales of the salmon belly, outlining with silver any islands floating in this river of light. The sky to either side of light path was indigo blue, a velvet dark broken only by pinpricks of stars bright enough to compete with a more seamless rush of moonlight.

Ruth had never seen a sky path this specific so near to earth. There had been nights when she stood under desert skies, slept on the high plains beneath the spinning river of the Milky Way, imagined herself walking its distance, spiraling out from its clutched center to the furthest edge where the paving stones of stars were spaced so far from one another that she would have had to leap centuries if she wanted to stay on the road, but this sky path was different, more accessible.

Then, imagining herself as a pilgrim wandering the Milky Way had been an approach to the impossible, a path to unknown futures. But this trail was attached however tenuously to the cliffs at the far back of the valley before speeding out to sea as a generous pathway where it tagged loosely to the horizon, moving up and down as if tugged by the tides, breathing in and out as if conscious of human breath. It was a pathway closer to earth than heaven, a bridge perhaps from here to there, a jumping off point, a way home, a skyway to somewhere. One wouldn't fly along this route as one might over the Milky Way. This salmon belly sky was an unpaved road, meant for hiking. She was sure there would be stopping off places where a hiker might lean on rough hewn rails and throw pistachio shells into sluggish waters below. She was equally certain that when the shells hit the water, fish would leap from the cross currents, leaving rainbow trails behind. She imagined an oasis at mid-journey, a marketplace, crowded improbably with camels laden with brightly colored silks, squat donkeys carrying bundles of twigs, lop-eared mules hauling tinkers' carts. Bells clanging, vendors of Qing Dynasty pots calling out their wares while pilgrims sat quietly in the much longed for shade of fig trees, spreading newly bartered honey on the dense bread they had carried from dark mountain valleys to this shimmering floating island oasis far out to sea, as far from any sense of beginning as it was from any practical ending.

The more Ruth thought of this imagined marketplace, balanced on light, the more she wanted to throw open her old sea trunk and find her gypsy scarves, her black and white jester's outfit, sew the bells back on, and take off laughing on the skyway to somewhere.

But not now.

Now, she had to keep putting one foot in front of the other and march down to the shore and check her nets. Hank, the self-appointed game-warden's assistant, that first-class pain in the neck, had come calling late in the afternoon to "inform her" that she didn't have a permit to set nets and if she didn't pull them in, he was going to call Captain Leroy first thing in the morning and Cap'n Leroy would tell her a thing or two. Leroy Jones was the real game warden, elected not appointed, and unlike Hank, he understood clearly that folk still fished out of necessity on this remote coast rapidly filling with high-priced houses and tourist hotels. She knew he would caution her in his nasal Midwestern whine about setting nets too close to shore, remind her that taking too tiny fish from the sea was bad ecological practice, but he knew she wouldn't do that. He knew she had to eat, and she wasn't going to eat if she didn't wait until big fish swam willingly into the net.

She had thought briefly about going down to City Hall and taking out a restraining order against Hank but what would she say? That he knocked on her door at least twice a week to remind her to cut the weeds out front, caution her about her nets, tell her that her garbage cans were disreputable? What would the judge say to that? Excuse me, Ms Renwick, that *is* your name is it not, might you consider that Mr. Fenway is simply being neighborly, reaching out a helping hand?

Of course, Ruth knew that the only place Hank wanted to put his helping hand was between her legs and help himself to something she didn't want him to have. Only after she had told him in no uncertain terms that she was not interested did Hank take on the role of concerned neighbor. Clearly, he was more interested in the shapeliness of her body than in the tidiness of her yard, but the law's the law.

She needed real cause to get a restraining order, and the "polite" actions of an overly concerned neighbor apparently were not cause enough. No matter. Ruth could take care of herself, thank you very much. Nonetheless, she certainly didn't need the town drunk knocking on her door every afternoon at sunset. She wondered what the judge would say if Hank knocked on his door to tell him his daughter's skirt was too short or that her red lipstick was unnerving. As an artist, Ruth appreciated eccentric behavior, but Hank wasn't eccentric. He wasn't even interesting.

She'd met many interesting people after leaving her job as curator of Chinese antiquities at the Boston Museum of Fine Arts. She'd left the East coast, roamed about the American west in her makeshift gypsy wagon. She'd met a lot of jerks, too. People tend to notice a young woman alone, hanging onto reins attached to the bridles of high-spirited horses moving along at such a clip that it might seem that the brightly painted wagon rolling behind was incredibly lightweight, filled perhaps with nothing but light, but she had her entire life in there, including a cook-stove made of a discarded 55-gallon drum.

Whenever she rolled into yet another small town far from the more determined hustle of the Eastern cities, those who believed that anyone who lived on the road had to be a drug addict or worse yet a murderer would march right up to City Hall and file their complaints. Then, the police would show up inquiring to see her machine gun, announcing in all seriousness that Sara Jane down at the Five and Dime had sworn she had seen two tommy-guns hanging off the back of her wagon. Ruth would invite the nervous young men with their shiny badges to inspect her shovel for any sign of a trigger. They might shrug apologetically, but within an hour, one or the other would be back with a search warrant because Elmer at the Hardware store had sworn he had seen her selling "magic" cigarettes to the kids in the playground. Once again, she would invite him in, asking only that he be sure to put everything back exactly as he found it and please be extra careful with her porcelain teapot. It had belonged to her grandmother.

After a few of these forays into her personal life, she learned how to pare down to bare necessities that could be openly displayed. She gave up drawers and cabinets because, of course, not one officer of the law ever put anything back. Eventually, after losing two pounds of Darjeeling tea leaves to a pimply policeman who had never seen bulk tea and couldn't tell the difference between oolong and ooh-la-la, she gave up the teapot, made tea forever more by the cup using teabags.

The summer of the gypsy wagon had been exciting at first, but she'd soon tired of small town America and made her way into the wide valleys of the Rocky Mountains, urging her horses over rutted roads that narrowed to trails. In the back of one such valley, just north of the New Mexico border, she set up camp in a sunny meadow next to an old trailer that looked abandoned. Even though there was an open-sided shelter at one end of the meadow that might have once been home to goats or sheep, it was obvious that if those dewy eyed bovines had once been at home there, they were no longer. There had been plenty of rain that year and the grass was knee-high, plenty for her horses to eat. Under cottonwood trees a short distance from the broken down trailer, she found a clear cold spring, and when she knelt to taste the water, she was surprised to see watercress and mint growing at its edges. The water was potable, and with the mint, she could make tea. Then, of course, she regretted giving up her teapot. It would have been lovely to sit on the stone near the spring, pouring thin green waterfalls of tea into her bone-china teacup balanced on her knee.

Ruth could have sworn that it was just at that moment, thinking about the teapot and reaching down to pick some mint, that the front door of the rusty trailer opened. The man who stepped out was as surprised to see her as she was shocked to see him, but any single woman who travels about in a gypsy wagon knows how to react peaceably and kindly, and Ruth was no exception.

"I was just thinking," she said, "I wish I still had a teapot."

The man's sun-lined face broke into a grin and he laughed the kind of low rumbling laugh that can only belong to a man who has more love in his heart than suspicion or mistrust. "I've got one."

When she stood, he lifted his hand, gestured for her to sit. "Wait, I bring it out. I have hot water inside. We'll sit by the spring, have tea, share the bread I baked this morning."

Ruth sucked her breath between her teeth. He wasn't inviting her in and didn't expect her to invite him. This was good. When he turned, she saw that his white hair had been braided into a long braid that reached nearly to his waist. When he returned, he had a sky blue linen cloth draped over one arm and on the other balanced an ebony tray, polished to a high sheen. Perfectly centered on the tray sat a purple teapot, its body carved with calligraphy and its handle shaped to mimic a tree branch with one delicate leaf still attached. He set the tray down gently on the wide flat stone next to the spring.

"Qing Dynasty?" Ruth felt she had to ask. "Shao Da Heng? Where on earth . . ."

"How did you know?" He spoke before Ruth had a chance to finish her second question, and before Ruth had a chance to answer his question, he thrust his hand towards her. "I'm sorry, I don't even know your name and you don't know mine. I'm Paul, and you?"

"Ruth." First names seemed fine for now. "So tell me, how do you come to have such a beautiful teapot here in this wilderness?"

"Ruth," he paused after filling the first cup with the transparent green tea. "If I tell you that, then you must tell me how you know that this teapot was made by Shao Da Heng."

Reaching for her teacup, she smiled. "Fair enough. These cups are beautiful but Ming not Qing."

Paul lifted his teacup with right hand and gently shook his head. "My goodness, you *are* a surprise."

"Oh, it's no mystery, really," Ruth sipped her tea. "I worked for years and years as a curator at the Boston Museum of Fine Arts."

"Ah, then," Paul was laughing now, "you *would* know this pot. It *belongs* to the Museum. I'm a restorer – that's my studio over there." Paul gestured towards the rusty trailer.

"Paul?" Ruth was looking more intently now at this smiling man, his sparkling eyes, his gentle hands. "Paul. Are you Paul High Eagle? Ruth Renwick."

"The one and the same, Ms Ruth Renwick, the one and the same." Now it was Paul's turn to stare at her, her long black hair tied back with a blue silk scarf, her pale skin, her bandaged leg.

"What are the chances? I can't believe this. This is just way *way* too strange. Impossible."

Ruth turned the now empty teapot over in her hands, and then she shook her head.

"You can't be Paul High Eagle. Why would the best restorer of Chinese ceramics and American Indian art be working out of a broken down trailer at the end of a dirt road in a valley where the snow is sometimes so deep that going in and out is impossible? That's what they told me in town. Three weeks, they said, three weeks and then you best high tail it out of there before the snows start. I don't believe you. I can't believe *this*. It can't be."

As it turned out, the white haired gentleman with the broken down cowboy boots and the broken down trailer was indeed Paul High Eagle. When Ruth refused to believe him, he went back into the trailer and brought out the letters she had written over the years, asking and then begging to come and visit his studio. He had always refused but then by some quirk of fate that neither of them could explain, here she was.

How she ended up on his doorstep, they both agreed was a question best left unanswered. Paul just shook his head and invited her in to see his workspace. After all, some mysteries deserve reward. Even before he opened the door to his studio, Ruth understood that Paul High Eagle was a true eccentric, his wobbly orbit capable of bringing him ever so close to the heart of culture and then far into the deep belly of country where few ever venture. She was sure that it was his keen sense of observation and wonder that allowed him equal access to both worlds, but she had to admit, his studio surprised her even more than their initial encounter.

Before opening the door he made her swear – truly swear – that she would tell no one about the studio, explaining that everyone in town thought he was just some crazy Indian driven mad by the white world. Half of the town folk were Apache and they could easily understand why some old Sioux would want to go live in a rundown trailer next to the best spring in the valley. Made sense.

He called himself Taylor Running Deer, bought a worn-out industrial strength treadle sewing machine and set himself up with a small business fixing bridles and belts, nothing fancy. Never accepted any work that was decorated with silver or turquoise, always made some excuse about his own clumsiness, not wanting to damage the stones, but in reality he just didn't want anyone rummaging about his trailer looking for enough silver to trade for beer down at the One Stop.

After a while, folks got the idea. That old Indian, they said, he just sews plain leather (no shimmer, no jingle, no shine) but his prices are okay and his work's decent. More than decent, they said, he's good. So, they brought their saddles, their holsters, and every few weeks a friend from Denver drove down in a beat-up pick-up truck to bring the real work, pieces sent by Boston Museum of

Fine Arts, the Museum of Natural History, the DeYoung, etc. Nobody knew what he really did and he wanted to keep it that way. He made her swear, clap her hands, turn three times around, and spit on the ground. Swear she would tell no one. Only then would he open the door.

When he did, papers lifted from the floor and blew in a strange frenzy before settling down on a threadbare sofa littered with beer bottles and empty frozen TV dinner trays. Appropriate. Made as much sense as an oversized TV, tuned to some Mexican soap opera, providing the only electric light. Exactly what one might expect to see in a beat-up trailer tilted into dead end of the valley. Next to the refrigerator, the soundless TV balanced precariously on a stack of moldering magazines that seemed quite at home in the sea of paper that flooded the room.

It was impossible to know if the room was carpeted or not, but she thought not as it appeared they were in the kitchen. Really, there was no way of telling. She was standing on such a thick layer of paper, glommed together with mud and goodness knows what else, every time she moved she was unsure whether she would drop through to the floor or the field below. Bills, advertising circulars, newspapers, paperbags. Who knew what slithered and skittered underneath all that paper. When Paul saw the shock register on Ruth's face, he laughed.

"Part of the stage set, my dear Ms Renwick." He threw his arms up and out. "If you were some old drunk looking for a few nickels to buy a bottle of rotgut, would you look here? Bet ya anything, you'd leave as quickly as you came. This mess keeps even the most brazen of thieves out of my studio."

Then he lifted the torn Army blanket hung in the doorway leading to what must have once been the living room or the bedrooms or both. They walked down a dimly lit narrow hall, passing closets overflowing with piles of towels, worn blue jeans and faded flannel shirts. At the end of that hall was another matted wool blanket stapled to the fiberboard ceiling and hanging inches above the trash-laden floor. Behind that blanket were several cinderblocks end to end on the floor – *Blocking the trash river,* Paul said – and then, another door, this one firmly closed. When Paul opened that door, Ruth saw a well-lit, neatly organized room, its windows blocked off with multiple layers of newspaper, nothing that would raise the eyebrows of anyone snooping about outside. Newspaper insulation was commonplace in backwoods trailers. Long immaculate counters of polished wood stretched the length of one wall and cabinets with glass doors covered the facing wall. At the far end of the counter were pieces of what appeared to be a Ming Dynasty bowl and in the middle, three very different moccasins, each beaded with porcupine quills. Next to the moccasins, a shallow tray filled with quills of different colors. Obviously, current projects.

They talked for hours that day and then she went back to her gypsy wagon and he to some space in the trailer where he slept, in a bed she never saw. He swore it was quite ordinary and quite comfortable, teased her to come and see, but she had kept her distance. She stayed on for a week or so and they often had tea in the afternoon, spoke about art and Chinese history, how the sea change of the tea ceremony during the Ming Dynasty had altered forever the design of cups and pots. Then one day, when the clouds seemed impossibly low, the air impossibly still, Paul had knocked on her door to tell her snow was coming and she'd best take her wagon back to town. They said their good-byes and she promised to come back next summer. He smiled, put her hand to his lips, and wished her safe travels.

The next summer, she did return but not in her gypsy wagon. She was through with that. She drove down from Denver in a rented car, muscled her way over the rutted road to the back of the valley, but when she came to the meadow, the trailer was gone. The flat stone lay untouched next to the cold clear spring, and the grass was as tall as ever. Still no critters living in the falling-down shelter at the far end of the meadow. On her way back to the highway, she asked down at the One Stop if anyone knew what had happened to Taylor Running Deer, but the man behind the counter just shrugged. *Them Indians,* he said, *they come they go.*

Someone else told her some computer billionaire who preferred not to be named had bought that whole end of the valley and everybody had to move on out. Back to the plains. Back to the cities.

Perhaps Paul's orbit and hers were so eccentric that they would only cross paths once in a thousand years. She never saw Paul again, and she really didn't understand why now, standing under this starry sky, thinking of him. Maybe he had gone off on the salmon belly cloud, a light path to somewhere, a jumping off point. There was no way of knowing. All she knew was that he had moved on and so had she. She hoped he wasn't dead, but if he was, she hoped he was walking on that light path, traveling on. Safe journey, Ruth said quietly to no one in particular before kneeling on the rocks and gathering her nets. No fish tonight.

Running with the Grunion

It was well after midnight when Laura stepped from the porch onto the cool concrete of the drive that looped behind the house, ending at a ramshackle building that might serve as a garage but as she had no car, that shack had become a combination garden shed and studio. One corner was stacked with terracotta pots and bags of rotting manure, opposite were her canvases and a long table where ruined tubes of paint lay scattered about.

A largish canvas, a portrait, balanced uneasily on her makeshift 2x4 easel. The painted image was as uneasy as the balance. In the past two days, she had wiped all features from the face again and again and again. It was hard to paint from memory those gentle eyes she had so loved. The face was now a pale pastel stain, crisscrossed by vague shadows of lines drawn and erased, every one judged too tentative to remain. The painting with its scrubbed out face was fast becoming a statement about removal and absence rather than the respectful and gentle portrait she had wanted, but she wasn't going to work on it tonight. Working under neon lights would just exacerbate the problem. If she were ever to find that face again, it would be in the early morning or in the pale reflected light of evening. Neon simply wouldn't do.

Above in the indigo sky, stars sparked and whistled – so numerous that they blurred together until islands of light appeared, looking like coastal cities seen from above, spreading outward like the fingers of sea creatures from dark seas to darker land. The Milky Way spilled as a wide river overhead, so fluid and lovely that Laura felt that if she only had a tiny bit more spring in her step, she might launch herself from her diving board driveway and fall gracefully upward into those luminous waves, but spring in her step was exactly what she was missing these days. She desperately missed diving into the sea. To dive into sky was simply not possible.

There had been years when she was living at her Grandmother's at the beach when the red tide would arrive, and after dark, the waves spilled phosphorescence onto sands already glittering with the nearly invisible diamonds of worn-down sea glass and shells. To swim in the red tide with those green-exploded waters had been a great joy. When she lifted her arms from the sea, curtains of light, so like fallen stars, wrapped her skin. Suddenly, she had Tinker Belle wings and bones as fragile as weightless as dust. She was sure that swimming the Milky Way would be like that, only grander and smoother.

And without the bits of sand.

Always, when the red tide came in, so did the grunion, thousands of slender fish dragging glowing lines of light from sea to shore as they flopped their way up the beach to drill holes and lay eggs. Racing to avoid the humans and their nets, a certain percentage never made it back to the sea, but some always did and she had been glad for that. There was something profoundly disturbing about wild whoops of glee as nets scraped across the sand to scoop dozens of egg-laying fish, something barbaric about killing creatures during such a vulnerable time. Everyone came down to the beach when the grunion rolled ashore. Acting every inch the great white hunter, her uncle had once cooked a massive breakfast of pan-fried grunion, bacon, and eggs. Not wanting to offend him, she placed one small crisped grunion on her plate and nibbled its white flesh, told herself she was eating fruits of the sea placed on glowing sand by night fairies, but the fish had been bland and bony and all she could think of was what it must have been like to die while performing rituals of procreation.

She never should have eaten that fish. Something from its untimely death insinuated itself into her flesh and left her gasping. Later, every time her now ex-husband had laid his hand on her thigh, she had thought of those slender fish, bathed in moonlight and washed by phosphorescence, valiantly making their way up the beach only to be scooped by a net or crushed by a shovel. Grunion runs hadn't much helped her marriage.

After Robert took off with the bartender from the Blue Whale down by the cove, Laura discovered she couldn't sleep in their great four-poster bed with its blue and white log-cabin quilt. Nothing strange about that really, but what was strange was that she also found that she could no longer sleep inside. She spent two months after his departure sleeping on the beach, inside the rhythm of the waves, watching stars disappear like grunion beneath blankets of fog and waking only to the whistle of the midnight train making its way up the coast.

During those days, color seemed warmer than any log-cabin quilt. Color twined around her; she slept easily in the orange heat of the day and spent her night singing to the stars. She fell asleep to the pale pinks of dawn and woke to the flaming red of evening, always glad for the blue blue blue of the sea and the green that crept down to the shore. Then, on day 63 of her life sleeping under sky wind and waves, her friend Sara had showed up with rope, threatened to lasso her if she didn't come along like a good little doggie, and so off she went.

She had stayed with Sara and Ray for a week or so before deciding to sell her house and move up the coast where there were still towns with falling down houses and wild land. After that, everything was smooth sailing. She sold the house for more than she had dreamed possible, and within a week, she had found this place with its wild rose garden, a dormant vegetable garden staked out with bamboo and the drafty cedar-shingle garage in the back, perfect for a studio. She would paint what she remembered.

The only problem with that notion was that her memory was as foggy as those first nights on the beach. If star paths had been obscured by sea fog, her recollections were obscured by anger confused by love. She managed a few small Frida Kahloesque pictures of traumatic events that had been previously well described by the telling and retelling of tales over and over and over. She had her own bright green mauve and purple miscarriage, tethered to thunder-studded sky by black-winged birds with outstretched wings and golden beaks. There was the motorcycle accident, flaming wheels flying like Van Gogh's crows over sun-dried valleys, littered with nuts, bolts, and axels. And her own wedding, modeled after the dour solemnity of Grant Wood's "American Gothic", except that the groom had a bloodied heart pinned to his lapel and stood staring at something well away from the borders of the picture while the bride clutched a slender silver fish to her breast, her eyes like rivers. It all seemed a bit over the top.

She had set out to paint reality and had ended up creating the most maudlin surrealité that when examined carefully and dispassionately had little or none of the poetry and pathos that Frida Kahlo infused in her paintings and even less of the extraordinarily detailed strangeness of Salvador Dali. Laura's color stumbled blindly against the poorly executed images, and anything elusive that might have sparkled like the sea sparkled on the nights of the grunion runs drowned in a hard-edged awkward intentionality that left the viewer feeling hopeless and stabbed. And maybe a bit bored.

The paintings were not successful, and Laura stacked them near the tomato cages, their garish colors facing the wall. She hadn't wanted to see them anymore, but was not yet ready to slash them from their stretchers and heave them into the trash. That seemed as brutal as scooping dozens and dozens of grunion from midnight sands without being hungry. Her paintings, after all, were like those fish, marching blindly from the sea, believing dumbly that such a march would guarantee further days beneath sunlit waves. The fish were blind; she was blind, but that didn't matter. She just needed to find a way to *see* and was confident that she could do just that. She would stop painting events and start painting faces.

That decision had been like opening a faucet. As soon as she had mouthed the word "portrait," energy poured through her like a riptide. She raced about, picking up weeks of newspapers strewn about the living room, washing stacks of dishes in the kitchen. She organized the bookcases, sorted the paints in the studio, swept the floors, vacuumed the rugs. Every weed in the vegetable garden was yanked and layered with lime in the composter, every rose neatly pruned. She harvested the last of the lemons and picked the one fig on the tiny tree she had planted when she first bought the house. She bought a new broom to sweep beach sand from the drive, a new nozzle for the hose to banish road grime the porch. She set the last of the fieldstones into the growing patio, humming while she worked. She never did learn how to whistle.

Her grandmother had been a portrait painter and as a child Laura had spent long hours watching as short lines and multi-colored dabs transformed pale ambiguous washes into a vibrant young mother holding a baby with skin as translucent as ice, cheeks like roses, paradise eyes, and a smile as warm as very first warm day of spring when suddenly there are flowers everywhere. That transformation from canvas to portrait more than amazed Laura; it fed her. Her grandmother had always wanted to paint like Mary Cassatt, to breathe life into eyes and skin, but her paintings, as tender as luminous as Mary Cassatt's, stayed in private collections, never found their way to museum walls. Grandma, Laura decided, would be her guardian angel, sitting on her shoulder, telling her how to mix the subtle colors of dawn, when to lift her brush, when to stop the line.

Of course, it didn't work out quite like that. Ghosts rarely show up when you need them. Laura was on her own and without the training her grandmother had had (she had been a student of Kokoschka), Laura had no idea where to start. She hung her grandmother's paintings on the wall of her studio and then sat for hours, hoping for "messages" but ended up napping while sitting in a straight-backed chair.

When she told Jane of her plan to paint portraits, Jane agreed to come and sit. Laura gave her straight-backed chair to her most willing model who sat and read as Laura worked all day. First, she outlined the head, marked the position of the hands, the tilt of the brow, dutifully building the painted surface stroke by stroke as she had seen her Grandmother do, but the resulting portrait held none of the soft velvet of Jane's eyes, nothing of the vivid tension of her bones.

Indeed, her pale blue eyes looked more like red-hot coals, rockets ready to fire out of her skull and bones seemed misshapen, even broken. Her quirky smile had resolved itself into a demonic grin. One casual dimple had morphed into a raw angry canyon, and her delicate ivory skin looked dangerously green.

Embarrassed by the failure of her efforts, Laura had pretended to slip on the greasy garage floor and spilled a jar of turpentine over the surface of the painting, necessitating a cleanup that served as useful erasure. Finally, Laura had to admit that blood didn't guarantee talent or skill. A painter's art doesn't descend through the genes. Rather, she thought, it's an art learned by the body schooled by the eye. She would have to paint what she saw.

Of course, that didn't quite work out either. Laura knew what she *wanted* to see and thought that what she wanted to see was indeed *what* she saw. As she painted, she painted through that film of desire, ignoring the gentle and somewhat sad blue shadow flushed across the brow of the face she painted, painting instead smooth flawless skin, blushed pink with a youth long gone. When she finished the portrait, she could see something had gone wrong, but could not understand what or why. Time after time, she scrubbed the portrait out. It hadn't worked to paint through memory or in imitation of another's style, and now, it seemed, her most original approach was failing as well. Finally, her patient model, her darling Jane, grew impatient, told Laura she had never been able to see her and never would, slammed out the door, and that was that. Now Laura was painting from memory and memory was yielding very little. This last scrub-out seemed permanent.

At midnight, watching the streetlights sigh behind the camellia bush, Laura breathed. Somewhere, blocks away, a siren wailed and a dog barked. Someone was awake and in trouble; one might look at it that way, or one might think that the siren was announcing the imminent arrival of help. Problem noted, help on the way. Such a world of difference between the two. The siren scratched across her skin, and she was glad when it finally faded to a thin tremor, replaced by the rustle of the wind as it lifted tree branches and pushed moonlit clouds across the sky. Somewhere nearby, perhaps beneath the porch light, a lizard chirped as if startled. Laura turned to look back at the porch and waited until she saw the lizard scuttle across the screen, a small black comma beneath the bare yellow bulb. Everything was wordless language – wind whispering, stars speaking, insects punctuating sentences spilled by birds half hidden by the dark green leaves of the camellia bush.

Some small creature, hidden either by the light or by the dark, uttered a sharp dry cry, a single note that opened the night in a way that the sirens had not. She waited to see if the creature would run out, if the bird would fly, but both settled back into the dark, as if evaporating, just as those grunion that escaped capture had settled back into the sea. Laura breathed again, this time deeper, fuller. She felt night move into her lungs, stars thread into her blood. Tomorrow, she would listen to the noises color makes, look for its edges, watch her heart, feel her breath. Tomorrow, she would begin to paint the in-between.

Harmonics

"What do you call a bird who loves to sing along with Mozart's Piano Fantasy in D Minor and squawks loudly if I pick up my guitar to practice?" Jerry flipped a pencil in Beth's direction, watched it bounce once on the rag rug, and then arc upwards before falling point down in the potted fern.

"A music critic with taste?" Beth allowed her voice to lift as if she were making a joke, but really she quite agreed with Sami Bird's assessment of Jerry's guitar playing. Ever since her brother had come to stay with her, she'd been listening to this bird-to-boy squabble. Secretly, even though Sami's strident squawks shook her world, she hoped the bird would win out in the end. Lately, she had found herself taking long walks along the forest trail simply because Jerry somehow understood chords as approximate, and as a result, much of his playing sounded like an aging semi-truck grinding through gears on a curving mountain road that had been blasted through rock. The echoes were not pleasing.

Lately, she'd been hoping that Jerry would find an apartment in town, closer to the clubs he loved, closer to his pals, closer to his work, but really, he had as much right to live here as she did. They had both grown up in this long-suffering house, nestled up against the mountain, so she supposed the rent was right. Just right for a poet and a struggling (truly struggling) musician. No mortgage and low low taxes, but also no landlord to call when the winds blew tree limbs onto the roof.

There's the rub.

Living in a house alone is a bit like burrowing into the belly of some great blundering blind outer space creature, mumbling incomprehensible code and quite incapable of feeding itself. The beast has to kept warm, dry, and well-fed if the stomach dweller is to live, but first it is necessary to translate and understand the odd words the house-creature barks out late at night when the winds are pushing in from the north, find at least some sense in the small squealing whimpers heard when the rains are steady on the roof. Forcing the house-beast to speak human talk just won't work. Creature consciousness is too different from human desire.

She had spent one whole winter lying awake listening to roof timbers scraping into the bones of the house, shifting corners and warping window frames. She had felt as if she were on a ship at sea but that the ship was sailing without a captain. On particularly rocky nights, she walked about checking windows and doors, feeling certain that soon they would blow out and she would be left exposed to winds. That never happened, of course, and by spring she had figured out through numerous conversations with those who understood old houses that post and beam houses, held together with pegs instead of nails, did shift about. This house was not a fortress, standing against the wind. Rather, it was a tango dancer, partnered with the wind. Its flexibility was probably the reason it was still here on this mountain after 250 years.

Years ago when she was still trying desperately to write a decent poem, Beth had lived alone on the coast of Maine in a small one room fishing shack. Her "house" had only been big enough to accommodate a single bed, a rickety table barely capable of supporting a typewriter, a chair, and a small wood-burning stove with enough room on top for a large frying pan or a tea kettle but never both together. The shelves surrounding the only window opposite the bed held books and jars filled with noodles, rice, tea and once bent now straight nails. A thick plush rug kept the wind from hissing through the floorboards and bright yellow oilcloth tacked over the north wall kept the wind from washing over her face as she slept. She was quite comfortable during the autumn months, spending her mornings writing and afternoons gathering blueberries growing along the path down to the beach where she kept her dinghy and her lobster trap. She was grateful to be finally away from the steamy and often angry competition of academe. She truly thought she had discovered an idyllic life, the perfect life for a poet, writing through her own conversations with the

Universe, living off the grid, eating nothing but rice, lobster and blueberries. A good diet.

When winter arrived with a fury she hadn't expected, Beth didn't feel any particular concern about the gale force winds that were piling great whitecaps on the sea below. She had stacked plenty of neatly split logs just feet from her front door and so could gather up armloads of wood, lay a crackling fire in the stove. Beth thought she might just drink a cup of green tea, wrap herself up in blankets and then meditate on the voice of the wind, listen for the whisper of God.

By midnight, she no longer felt so brashly confident.

If the wind was speaking with God, this god was hugely irrational. The wind had moved from howl to hysteria and the corrugated tin roof was heaving upward as if pulled by a very large magnet attached to some UFO hiding inside the storm. It was all she could do to keep the stove cranking out enough heat to take the edge off the frigid winds that were briskly whistling through new or previously undiscovered cracks in house walls. She imagined that soon that the entire house would take off across the field, sliding to the edge of the cliff like Charlie Chaplin's cabin in "Gold Rush."

She thought twice about just abandoning ship, but each time she opted to stay, imagining that the blinding snow would make any movement next to impossible. Negotiating even something as relatively simple as the hundred yards or so to her beat-up pick-up parked near the road would necessarily be treacherous. By dawn the storm had abated somewhat, but the roof was gasping and sighing, lifting ever so slightly with every breath of wind.

When the wind suddenly changed direction, she had heard a pop-pop-popping and a thin rasping of metal creasing metal. When the room grew brighter she knew what had happened, one section of the tin roof had peeled away and she was suddenly inside the storm. Then, her personal debate ended. She picked up her typewriter and her two extra pairs of woolen socks, stuffed them together with her manuscript into a backpack and headed out the door, forging a path through blinding snow towards her truck.

That Beth made it to the truck was as much the result of luck as determination, but she didn't know how to assess the measure of either. She was just glad to be once again out of the wind and inside a space with a roof. She would have to wait for the snowplow, of course, but once it came, she knew what she would do. She would fire her ratatat baby up, follow closely behind the slow-moving truck until she reached the highway, then turn south and drive nonstop home to Virginia, which is exactly what she did.

Eight years passed since Beth's experimental north woods hermitage, and now, she supposed, it was Jerry's turn to try his luck with artistic loneliness, only he wasn't alone. He was here with her, camped out in his old childhood room, cranking up his electric guitar and asking her what she was planning for dinner as if the passing years had reinvented her as their dead mother and father rolled into one.

Beth supposed that was her own fault. After all, when she had learned of the plane crash, she'd rushed home from med school (another ship abandoned) and dedicated herself to preparing breakfast and dinner for Jerry until he was old enough to go to boarding school. It was then she had shuttered the house and taken off to her coastal hermitage hoping to write if not the great American novel at least a minor American poem. That she hadn't was no great loss. She was glad she had come home.

Of course, it was ironic she had to come home to discover the joys of solitude, but finally she was happy here, puttering about in her gardens, sitting with Sami Bird on the porch her father had built overlooking the creek below. At first, she thought she would just fix things up a bit, sell the house and move on, but when winter slipped into spring, she thrilled to see the daffodils push up through the dark soil near the creek. On her seventh birthday, Beth and her mother had planted each of those bulbs together. Her mother had shown her how deep to dig each hole, how to plant each bulb root side down, and most importantly how to imagine how each flower would fit into the forest glade, how to make sure each would find enough sun to grow and bloom. Together Beth and her Mom searched the creekside for places where low growing plants grew easily and sturdily, then lay flat on their backs and looked up to see where the sky seemed widest and bluest between the spreading trees. There they had planted the bulbs. That afternoon still played like a movie inside her head.

Every day that spring some little thing she noticed or passed by started yet another movie reel rolling – the notches carved on the edge of the bathroom door, each neatly labeled in her father's careful cursive with the year and her name or Jerry's, tiny handprints in the concrete out back, her mother's climbing rose planted from a cutting her sister had sent from Britain. By the end of the summer, she knew she wouldn't sell the house. How could she sell the dam she and Jerry had built the summer of the plane crash, a dam that had held all these years since, holding behind it just enough water to create a swimming hole and allowing the excess to tremble over its lip in a gossamer mist that attracted dragonflies and hummingbirds?

"*What?*"

Jerry was yelling something below, but Beth couldn't make out the words. She strained to hear but his words were muffled by closed doors and altered by bird song filtering through open windows.

"I can't hear you, Jerry. I'll be right down."

Beth hadn't hesitated a minute when Jerry had called and mumbled something about wanting to come home. It had taken him some time to get around to asking. He spoke first at length about his studies, then the band and the mishaps of their last gig. He kept her laughing, telling one funny story after another until finally he just stopped talking. At first she thought the phone had gone dead, but she realized that if she listened very carefully, she could hear street noise, dogs barking, garbage cans clanking, busses starting up and stopping. When a siren rose and passed, she grew concerned, but then, Jerry cleared his throat – loudly, just as their father used to do – and began to talk rapidly about their childhood, about Mom, Dad, Cyrus their dog.

There were no spaces between his words, and just when she thought he would surely run out of breath, he said quickly *I want to come home,* and, without missing a beat, she had said *of course.* Jerry, she knew, would discover what she had found after coming home. He would find the same peace in the echoes and shadows of their Mom and Dad. They would be a family again.

She forgot, of course, about the guitar or somehow assumed it didn't matter. She forgot she no longer needed or wanted to be mother to her brother, that she needed instead her solitude if she wanted to finish her book. She would have to tell him. She was losing traction. Some mornings she wrote nothing.

Jerry was yelling again, but he was closer. She could hear his boots on the stair. "I'm coming, Jerry. Just need to finish this sentence." The last wasn't true, of course. She had been dreaming not writing, but she needed to remind herself about writing. She glanced at her watch. Half past twelve. "I'm coming."

"Get your shoes, Sis," Jerry was leaning against the hall wall, his mouth folded into an easy grin. "I made lunch but I want to show you something first." He held the door open for her and then gestured towards the front door. "Outside."

He started off down the path leading to the vegetable garden and then veered off into the old pasture, heading for the abandoned horse barn. On either side of them, the meadow grasses grew tall, their feathered tips mixing easily with the last of the Queen Anne's lace and the dry stalks of chicory that only this morning had been covered with blue flowers. That this path was relatively new was obvious but that it was well used was also obvious. They walked on grasses that had been roughly cut down when they were near full growth but those stalks had dried and, in some cases, were trampled to dust. When they neared the barn, the first thing Beth noticed was fresh paint.

"Madame," Jerry bowed low, his right hand sweeping the ground in an exaggerated gesture. "Entrez, s'il vous plait."

The barn was a barn no longer. Inside was a simple but comfortable living space with a couch, chairs neatly placed around a raw wood table, a single floor lamp and a remarkably silent generator positioned just outside a large window that opened onto the forest beyond. A counter ran across one side of the room close enough to a brand new propane refrigerator and a two-burner camp stove that might make cooking possible if not easy. A narrow stair led to an open-sided platform built into the rafters, an oil lamp suspended below. Beth could see the edges of a bright blue futon with red wool blankets folded on top, Jerry's leather jacket hanging neatly from a hook on one wall. Beneath the stair were bookcases, already filled with books, and in one corner of the large downstairs room, Jerry's guitar rested against a truly portable amp, attached to its very own battery. Everything was crisp and clean, fresh white paint and vases overflowing with the last of the wildflowers and the first of the red gold leaves.

"Well?" Jerry was looking at her quizzically. "How do you like my new studio?"

"It hums, Jerry," Beth smiled softly, "and the echoes are round."

"Well, my dear sister, you sit here by the window and have a bite of this round." Jerry flipped open the white cardboard box on the table and pulled out a pizza. "I intend to get a better cook stove soon, a real stove, maybe even a solar oven, but today this is it. Pepperoni and mushroom! Hooray for take-out! Soon, Beth, soon, I'll have real electricity run back here, a gas stove for heat and hot water. We'll keep the generator next to the main house, your house, Beth, in case lightning strikes twice."

Beth folded her pizza, took a bite. Jerry was a better hermit than she had ever been.

Transplanting Family Trees

At this hour of the morning, the air was still cool and the spreading live oak trees, dripping with Spanish moss, swelled with the chatter of birds. Sophie liked rising before the sun and walking the three miles or so out to the highway. There was no reason to go, no newspaper delivery, no mail to pick up. She just enjoyed tangles of dawn, still thick with night fevers, leaking from surrounding swamps, mists that would thin by nine a.m., leaving the air empty, dusty and dry, ready for afternoon heat. Her bare feet made no sound on the white sand road and often she saw raccoons and other small critters dart out from under the palmettos and scurry from one side of the road to the other, preferring the confusion of the hammock land to the brief openness of the road.

Once a bobcat had crossed her path, stopping no more than three feet in front of her, dead center in the road. She stopped when the bobcat stopped and stood perfectly still, barely breathing. As if listening, the big cat turned its fringed ears toward her, and then, without moving his head, looked her up and down. She could feel his eyes touch her scalp and then move downwards over her neck, her arms, her breasts, resting briefly on the delicate skin of her belly, bare beneath the rolled edge of her chopped T-shirt.

She felt no fear; his golden eyes moved like water, and she was refreshed in that wild gaze. When he had finished looking, he padded off, disappeared into the underbrush and was gone. That day, Sophie hadn't gone any further down the road. When the bobcat left, she just sat down in the middle of the road, closed her eyes and listened, hoping to hear the forest whistle in response to the bobcat moving beneath the sweet gum trees, but she heard nothing that would alert her or any other creature to the bobcat slipping between the holly bushes and down past the swelling cypress knees at the edge of the lake. No cracking of twigs. No sudden flutter of wings. Scrub jays cried out, but their cries were not unusual. Frequently at dawn, they called to one another. At first their raucous calls sounded far apart, then closer closer closer until the awkward grey blue birds, gabbling loudly with one another, settled on the sturdy branches of the tallest live oak nearest the house. The gathering of the tribe, she called it.

This morning the air was particularly polished, almost blue in its stillness. Not a breath of wind. She wondered if that meant thunderstorms by afternoon. Even after two months of living down in this hammock land, Sophie was still figuring out the weather, still learning how much of this landscape was wilderness and how much was the dregs of civilization gone wrong. She was more interested in the surprising pink feathers of the Spoonbill than in the fact that the rotting timbers of the submerged docks, locked between the cypress knots, made perfect lounging holes for alligators, and she wasn't interested at all in the juvenile alligator who trundled up from the mud every afternoon in search of his daily dose of frozen food.

Six days after she and Margie moved in, the neighbor who leased the orange grove out by the highway had come by with a six-pack of Budweiser and some alligator jerky – at least that is what he said it was, might as easily have been salmon or salt pork for all she knew. He didn't even wait for them to invite him in, just opened the screen door and walked right in like he'd been doing it all his life, and for all she knew, that might just have been the case. Anyway, he plopped himself down at the kitchen table, offered the six-pack to Margie like it was a bottle of champagne and started to talk about how the previous owners, Jim and Rayanne, used to feed a baby alligator that was born down by the submerged dock. At first they were feeding him sardines, but then frozen smelt, the same stuff he and his buddy used for bait when they went fishing over in the Gulf.

After he had polished off three of the beers, Margie looked at Sophie and started talking as fast as she could in Polish, and Sophie responded with nonsense words. Even after all those years living on the circus lot, Sophie understood only English. The whole time they were carrying on this make-believe conversation, Margie kept glancing at her Dad's collection of supposedly razor sharp swords, scattered all over the kitchen table. They hadn't finished unpacking, but one of the first cartons they had unpacked had been Margie's "legacy," her Dad's swords used in his sideshow act when he was billed as "Mr. Slovatzny, The Greatest Magician and Sword Swallower This Side of the Mississippi." Didn't matter if they were east or west, that billing was always sensible.

After Margie let her eyes linger on the longest and perhaps sharpest of the lot, which was duller than a butter knife, she licked her finger, and then glanced back at Jeb or whatever his name was, touching her throat, all the time talking louder and louder until whatever she was saying sounded like a freight train about ready to bust off the tracks at a hairpin turn.

Sophie grabbed her arm now and again, then put her hand over her heart the moment Margie's eyes fluttered over to the fireplace where Sophie's "legacy" lay on the hearth stones – two highly polished starting pistols that her own father had held high overhead while putting his Lipizzaners through their paces in the center ring. When Margie began gesticulating wildly, Sophie made it seem as if she was making every effort to restrain her, and then when Margie's eyes lit on those pistols, Sophie let out a high-pitched yelp, kicked over the kitchen chair in her supposed haste to get to the guns before Margie did. It was constructed chaos, but if the construction went unrecognized, the chaos hit target.

At the moment Sophie leaped, the good ole boy, Jeb or what ever his name was, slammed out the screen door as fast as he had slithered in. They hadn't seen him since. She and Margie had laughed for hours. They poured the cheap beer down the sink and opened the champagne that they had bought after leaving Madison Square Garden in NYC after hearing the house was really and finally theirs. They would have a place to stay this winter and every winter in the near and far future.

Margie was a "web girl," an acrobat who performed on the web during spec when all eyes focused not on the center ring but on the track that surrounded all three rings, but she also had her own act performing all kinds of spectacularly scary tricks on a single trapeze without a net. The trapeze was her love; the web her necessity, part of the job. The "web" was just another name for long ropes hanging from the ceiling of the arena. As those ropes were as much of a platform for extravagance as was a spider's web, "web" seemed appropriate, especially as the women who performed there worked hard to entice their prey. Scantily dressed girls, including Margie, would shimmy up the ropes and then perform acrobatic acts that usually required them to open wide their legs and roll their heads back until their hair (or hair piece) flowed like waterfalls toward the sawdust below. Usually some gentleman – another performer, a clown, a juggler, an equestrian – made up to look like some theatrical swell in a Top hat, would stand below, polished black boots planted on the track, gently turning the rope so the girls could swing in easy orbits as they stretched and tumbled with the rope as their only support.

The circus was the great family sex show, Sophie's father had always said. He'd wanted Sophie to join him and his world famous Lipizzaner stallions in the center ring, but Sophie had decided she needed her own act. Working with her stepmother didn't seem like a brilliant idea. On her fourteenth birthday, Sophie decided to become a snake charmer, and she had enjoyed her act for years and years as a star performer of the sideshow, working the crowd from a small stage between the World's Tallest Man (he *was* tall, very tall, almost 8' tall) and the World's Fattest Woman (she was huge, very huge, with an uncountable number of folds of skin and fat). Sophie even threw in a belly dance or two on nights when the townies seemed particularly green and drunk enough to empty their pockets on the stage if her biggest boa yawned.

The snakes lived on the train with her, easily curled in their custom-made boxes, some with windows, some without. The boa constrictors, in particular, had been good pals, but then some well-meaning church ladies in one of those pale Midwestern town outside Chicago had decided that sideshows were shockingly demeaning and gathered up enough signatures to convince circus management, always nervous about how public perception might influence the nightly take, to close down the sideshow and "liberate" those poor down-trodden tall men, fat women, sword swallowers and snake charmers. Margie's dad lost his job, went back to Poland, and Sophie had no choice but to become a web girl.

Unfortunately, unlike Margie, Sophie didn't have the skills that might allow her to show off on a single trapeze doing the kind of tricks that made the audience gasp. Sophie wasn't really wasn't much of an acrobat (the real reason she didn't join her father in the center ring with the Lipizzaners). She just did her bit on the web as best she could and sold tickets for extra cash, sometimes with her oldest and most docile snake draped around her neck, until the church ladies put a stop to that as well.

Without her own act, Sophie was a bit bored, and when Little Jimbo, the elephant boy, told her that his folks were selling their bit of hammock land in central Florida, she had swallowed twice and asked Margie if she might be interested to go in with her and buy the place, mumbled something about raising chickens. To her great surprise, Margie had agreed and when the season ended, they just drove right on down and moved in. Just like that. They had three bedrooms – one for all their gear and one for each of them – two living rooms, and a big sprawling kitchen equipped with a real icebox and a woodburning cookstove. No electricity. They didn't need any. This was the opposite of the road; this was the land.

After they moved in, Sophie had decided she would write and Margie had decided she would perfect new tricks on her trapeze. She rigged her trapeze on the tallest live oak tree out near the turn in the road where Sophie had seen the bobcat that morning some weeks back, and while Sophie walked and scribbled, Margie worked out high above the white white sand. Originally, they thought when the day grew hot, they would swim in the smooth still lake out in front of the house but after the alligator tale, they'd decided that might not be wise. Instead they sat every afternoon on their slumping porch and watched the water, hoping to see the double black hyphens breaking the water, signaling the presence of one gator or sometimes two. They saw more giant egrets stepping delicately over the drying mud, dipping their heads to scoop minnows from the shallows, than they saw alligators, but they kept looking. Sophie she might coax one ashore, and then she might have the bare beginnings of a new act, Gal and Galloping Gator.

This morning when the sun was finally crawling above the tops of the pigeon plums that clustered near the edge of the orange grove, Sophie knew it was time to turn back. No bobcats today. She was more than a little disappointed that no critters had come out to meet her. She hadn't even seen the mama possum who usually trundled across the road about halfway between the highway and the house. Oh well. Sophie dug her heel in the white sand and dragged her foot into a wide circle. *Step here* she said. *Wild deer step here. Please.*

Margie would be just about finished with her morning routine on the trapeze, ready for a cup of tea and some of Sophie's famous flapjacks. Nearing the turn in the road where the great live oak grew, where Margie had rigged her trapeze, Sophie called out, letting her voice snap into the rising heat, and was surprised to hear Margie call back, not a greeting but a warning.

The next thing she knew, she heard a deep-throated bellow. If she were ever asked to describe that sound she would have had to describe it as red, rough, as large. As hollow as the empty arena after the show and as ornate as a circus wagon wheel. That roar had spangles in its interior. She stopped and stood as still as she had when the bobcat had whispered across the road, and what happened next, made her heart pound so fast she thought she would faint. She might have, too, if she hadn't been used to wrapping snakes around her shoulders.

Out from beneath the saw palmettos crawled an alligator larger than any she had ever seen in pictures, in the zoo, on the show, anywhere. When its giant snout was poking at the brush on the one side of the road, its roughshod tail was still concealed by the drooping leaves of the palmetto on the other side of the road. When it had all four feet on the flat white sand of the road, it suddenly turned that wideboard snout with its snaggle teeth to one side, shook its tail with such power she felt sure it would uproot the palmetto above it.

She couldn't help herself. She cried out. Fortunately, the swamp creature didn't seem to hear her, or if he did, he wasn't much interested. Heaving his belly from the ground, he propelled himself with a steely speed down the road away from her. She was amazed by how fast he ran. She could have sworn he was moving as fast as any deer. So much for barefoot circle spells of *deer step here*. As fast as the giant armored beast had appeared, it was gone. Just like Jeb.

Later, Margie told her that the old Methuselah alligator had crawled out of the brush as she was working her way through her second routine. She looked down and there he was – his old yellowed teeth pressed into his leathery jaws. At first she was fascinated by his hugeness. After all, she was in the air, perfectly safe. Unlike bears, alligators stayed horizontal, married to the ground. When he just shuffled over and lay down in strip of sun beneath the trapeze, she realized she didn't know how long he intended to stay and wondered how in the world she was going to get down, but that wasn't what bothered her the most. She started to worry about Sophie, wished she had something to throw, but she never worked with shoes and today was her day for simple routines. No Batons. No fans. The only thing she had to throw was her voice.

She reached deep into her lungs and screamed as load as she could, hoping she sounded like a panther or a lioness in heat, but that old guy either didn't or couldn't hear her. He melted onto the warm sand and closed his eyes. When Sophie called out, when Margie called her warning to Sophie, he moved his head. Who knows? Maybe, Margie said later, the old guy *did* hear Sophie and that's why he took off running. They didn't debate it long. Sophie was relieved that he hadn't decided to run after her, and Margie was ever so glad that she could finally climb down the rope and leave the trapeze empty. Together, they walked back to the house and had toast for breakfast. Sophie forgot about the pancakes but did squeeze fresh orange juice from the oranges she had pilfered from the trees in the grove. She never told Margie that she had lobbed one orange at the back of the fleeing alligator. She missed. Maybe the possum would find the orange and come to greet her tomorrow morning.

Rivers

"It doesn't seem 'ele-Gent.'"

Martha had our father's bone-thin arm cradled in her palm, and she was using her thumb to probe the veins creased into shallows of his inner elbow. Of course, she meant 'eligible,' and I knew that, but somehow 'eligible' had married into the clan of 'elegance' and reemerged as 'ele-Gent' with a soft 'g' as in 'gentle' or 'gentleman,' its hard edge being that tough clipped 'T' on the end of 'gent,' only by being chopped off at the knees, which made picture-perfect sense to me. Losing his language as he had in the last stages of Alzheimers, our father, a perfect gentleman, a writer all his life, had been cut off at the knees. I understood what Martha meant; it made sense that the delivery system bringing food to the brain would be suddenly no longer eligible, elegant, or ele-Gent. His brain was starving, apparently. At least that is what Doctor Patcher had said last week. No more wings for this gentleman.

Martha, of course, didn't mean any of that. That was me, entirely, making it real, finding something to hang on to. She'd just garbled the word as she always did. I wouldn't exactly call Martha Miss Malaprop, but she came pretty damn close. Once, I called her after she had taken her exams for her RN and was working the late night shift in the emergency room at Queens Hospital in Honolulu, six thousand miles away. I wanted to congratulate her, tell my sis how much I loved her, how proud I was of her, gush on about her pearly future, but instead, stupid me, I just asked how she was doing, how she was living. I know exactly what she said. How could I forget?

She said she was living 'slenderly.' She meant 'simply,' but that's not what I heard. In that word 'slenderly,' I found 'splendidly' waltzing peacefully with 'tenderly.' Such a life was just what I had hoped for Martha – to live splendidly and tenderly awash with sun and brushed by sea, and here she was, doing just that. I was ecstatic, but I'm afraid she was rather confused by my enthusiasm, and her surprise, of course, confused me. Later – years later – she explained that she had been trying to tell me as succinctly and as gracefully as possible that it might be nice if I could send her a few dollars now and again as she was still being paid apprentice wages and my business was thriving.

I was an importer back then, importing hand-painted doll heads from Taiwan which were then attached to rag bodies hand-sewn in Nicaragua and dressed up in sweet but extraordinarily detailed outfits (mainland China) before being sold at a huge mark-up to various high-end department stores. A few sold as dolls destined to live in playrooms, but most went to professionals who wanted representative dolls for office shelves, boardroom conference tables, hallway display cabinets. Lawyer dolls, Accountant dolls, Teacher dolls. That sort of thing.

Back in the nineties, when credit was flowing like water, back when everybody thought themselves millionaires or at least lived as if they were, back before the dams broke, I was selling these tiny little Frankensteins by the hundreds and making thousands. I had acres of money – enough to buy a three-bedroom condo on the upper west side of Manhattan, enough to fly to the Bahamas every winter, to the high reaches of the Alps every summer. I could have sent Martha checks so large she might have used them as shovels to dig her way out of the pile of school debt she was sitting on. Had I known, had I thought, but I didn't.

Instead, I imagined her living splendidly and tenderly. Instead, I sent her my best Nancy Nurse doll – a brunette wearing a removable monogrammed genuine white cashmere sweater with a tiny stethoscope spilling from the over-sized pocket of her 100% cotton uniform worn over silk stocking legs slipped into the most delicate glove-leather pumps. One gorgeous nurse, looking just like my gorgeous sister. I imagined that when Nurse Nancy arrived, Martha would call to tell me how nicely she fit in her new tenderly splendid life, how all the other nurses had clucked and cooed over Nurse Nancy's real human hair, but in fact, Martha didn't call.

Indeed, she didn't speak to me for years after that, hung up on me every time I called. To say I missed something basic would be an understatement. Language – as sharp as a scalpel. Life-giving, yes, but also, I suppose, potentially fatal.

"Ele-Gent." I let the word roll in my mouth. "What exactly do you mean?" I wasn't going to make the same mistake twice, let one of Martha's words roll away with my meaning attached.

"Nothing's flowing, Sam. I can't insert an IV, can't find my way in. This vessel's a mess; that one looks like a dried earthworm. Nothing's as it should be. Nothing eligible for entry." Martha paused. "Did I say ele-Gent? I meant, eligible. Senior moment, I guess."

Dad's pushing ninety, and we're both officially senior citizens, eligible for Social Security but still working, although our financial positions, if you want too call them that, have been neatly reversed. Martha's the one making decent money now, and I'm just shuffling along, teaching entrepreneurship as an adjunct at the local community college, which is somewhat of a joke because I'm not an entrepreneur anymore. Working as a teacher, it takes me a year to make what I once made in month. My business, not surprisingly, fizzled and flopped. Me teaching entrepreneurship? Who are we kidding? Who am I to tell enthusiastic young people how to run a business?

When the economy collapsed, so did I. When everything went ka-blooey, there were no accountants nor lawyers who would want to buy a hunky doll with male pattern baldness, wearing a hand-tailored suit and carrying a snakeskin briefcase that opens to reveal a miniature laptop that actually worked. Hot seller when things were popping in the eighties and nineties, but when businesses were following one another like lemmings over crumbling cliffs, no one wanted to be reminded of the excesses that pushed them to the edge of those cliffs.

When "Dolly Dearest" finally went under, I had a whole pallet of those lawyer/accountant dolls with their determined smiles and dark piercing eyes. Then, after selling all the wardrobe changes –

the mini straw hats and board shorts meant for summer holidays in the Hamptons – to a doll manufacturer in the Bronx, I made a deal with the bankruptcy judge to donate my remaining stock to various charities in exchange for some debt forgiveness, allowing me to avoid the long-term horror of bankruptcy but leaving me penniless anyway. I suppose some poor disturbed kid in South Brooklyn is filling that mini-briefcase with gold paper stars and fashioning paper sailor hats for the balding accountant doll, or maybe some down on his luck real-life accountant has pinned his ex-boss' name to the front of that very same doll that's now bristling with straight pins. Who knows? What the hell does any of that matter now?

I'm watching Martha, her hand on Dad's forehead. Her fingers are fragile butterflies, fluttering above his so blue eyes, bluer now that they have become so absent. When I look into that blue, I don't see him anymore. I see only the same kind of distance that keeps the sky so achingly far away. Martha's so gentle. Instead of make-up, she has kindness washed over her face – kindness leaking from smile creases around her eyes, kindness painted on her lips like some indelible glow-in-the-dark lipstick.

I recognized her at the airport because of that kindness. I wouldn't have known her otherwise – my own sister grown old, too much for me, I guess. When she called me, asked me to come, I wasn't sure I could come, wasn't sure if it was a good idea for the nasty old dragon to return to the fold, especially as that dragon was pretty bedraggled and down on his luck, tattered wings and all that, but when I walked down that airport hallway and saw Martha, more radiant than ever, her long grey hair loose on her shoulders, I knew I was okay. Her wings would lift me. She just opened up her arms and wrapped me up in all that kindness. I don't know where it comes from and I don't care. I'm just glad to be in that river.

Martha tells me that it won't be long, that when Alzheimers patients finally fall into complete unresponsiveness, when the eyes go blank, when the face settles into an immovable mask, then the brain is inches from shutting down the organs that keep the body alive. Dad no longer has any normal reflexes and his muscles seem more and more rigid every day. He doesn't know me, and that's okay, but it's tough that he doesn't smile. He can't laugh at any of my lame jokes, and his head stays upright only because I helped Martha fashion a foam-rubber cushion collar. She has some idea that he enjoys sitting at the window, and I guess if I were in his shoes, I'd like to sit there, watching the harbor. If he can still see, we want him to be able to see the waves spill across the rocks. I hope he hears the waves, the boat whistles, the birds in the ancient tree out front.

Sometimes, in the late afternoon when Martha's at work and I'm alone with Dad, I sit and tell him unadorned stories about my life. I figure that's the least I can do – share with him all those emotional up and downs that I so pointedly edited out in my gilded serialized life story I used to send to family every Christmas, cutesy tales printed on holly decorated stationary – me and the kids, me and the dog, that sort of thing. It may be too late, but now in the still of the afternoon, I can tell him the value of the small little things he taught me and gave me when I was a kid, how all his little homilies helped me throw away that heavy mantle I had carted around for so many decades when I thought I was thriving as an ironic businessman. I can tell him how his unbending love helped me find a way to walk with the rhythms of the earth instead of clomping around on top of them. I don't know if he hears me, and if he does, I still don't know if he cares about my grim little tales – his eyes never glimmer or move, his muscles are more stable than the reef out front. I blather on anyway, telling him how much I love him and massage his neck slowly and softly as Martha showed me how. I am a slow lizard on the rock of his back.

I wonder – I do wonder – what it is to turn to stone. I wonder if he still feels, and if he does what it must be like to feel and have no way to express that feeling. Does the feeling deepen, grow so intense that it overtakes the soul, or does the feeling efface until it drifts away like some spiderweb caught by a brisk wind heading out to sea? Is he at peace, colored as blue inside as his eyes are on the outside, or is his mind raging red at his unresponsive body, struggling to find a way out, to slip like fire through some small crevice to the world outside? Is he somewhere in there finding a wordless consciousness that I can't know but he cherishes with his bones? I wonder but I can't wonder aloud. I can't bother him with my stupid rhetorical questions. Instead, I cover his hand with mine and we sit quietly, listening to each other's breath as the sun falls to red and night comes on strong. Everyday when Martha comes home, she and I lift Dad out of his chair and lay him gently in his bed, wish him pleasant dreams. That ritual ends our day.

Martha brushes Dad's hair from his forehead, and I squeeze the water from the washcloth. "Martha?" I hold the damp cloth out to her.

"Thanks, Sam."

"Yesterday morning, early while you and Dad were still sleeping, I saw the most extraordinary sight. Not wanting to wake you guys, I made myself a pot of tea, went out on the lanai. Felt good to be bathed in the new pink light. I was looking past the point, watching the waves spark, when I noticed this silver fan appear above the darkest patch of water. At first I thought it was a sail, but it evaporated, disappeared as fast as it had appeared. I was curious and a bit confused, but then another phantom sail appeared and disappeared. Even before the great black bodies propelled themselves upwards into the new light, I had figured out I was looking at whales – many whales. Judging by the number of spouts, there had to have been at least eight or ten whales traveling together."

"Wow, Sam," Martha was looking at him and smiling, "you're lucky. I haven't seen one whale all season and you get to see a whole pod."

"Oh, Martha, there's more. As the horizon deepened into that shade of blushed pink that turns the sky above to turquoise green, I looked as I always do past that to the furthest horizon, but this morning instead of empty yet shimmering water, I saw more spouting. At least, two more pods, further out, and another closer in. Watching the, I felt incredibly hopeful. Years ago I was thrilled when I saw one whale and two made my heart race, but here were not just one dozen but several dozen, maybe more. There were great distances between the pods, but I swear to you, they were all traveling together. Changed the way I looked at the sea. Suddenly those vast expanses could be slipped into a thimble."

The whole time I've been talking, Martha's washing Dad's face, smoothing the sea-green washcloth into the crevices beside his nose, behind his ears, gently massaging his cheeks in small circles, then letting her palms flatten across the rigid muscles of his neck, fingers curling against his marble spine. Nothing changes with Dad's mouth; it stays closed. Nothing changes with his eyes, except they close. She kisses him gently, but the eyes don't flutter open. She's not the princess whose kiss awakes the frog, and I'm not the prince whose kiss can wake Sleeping Beauty in her glass coffin. The sleeping one stays asleep.

"Sam, give me a hand here. Dad's ready for bed."

Lifting Dad was like lifting a delicately carved statue of an upside-down tree stump. We had to be careful of the rigid but fragile roots – his arms, his legs – reaching past decades into the tangle of our shared lives. We didn't want to break anything. Roots matter.

What am I saying here? Who do I think I am? He's not a statue; he's not a stump. He's not a fancy dressed doll, a reminder of something that once was. He's our father and he's in there somewhere, watching us, feeling us, knowing us in the same way we know him, through our bones, our blood, our hearts. I know because I saw the whales dance. I know because, like Jonah, I was swallowed by those whales, sucked through sunlight to the wide river beneath the waves, mapped and navigated by the whales, a river that flows from here to there, touching the shores of everything that lies between.

Good night, sweet prince, good night.

Learning to Fly

By midnight, Jonah could tell that the waves were breaking further from shore. The heaving thrumming, the sometimes almost metallic crashing, had changed to a still heavy but gentler rhythm. He knew by morning sand would cover the exposed and broken coral reef out front. For days he and his little Jessica had picked their way across the rough and tumble coral, balancing first in hollows large enough to accept both feet before looking for a rock flat enough to serve as a stepping stone or better yet a bit of sand nestled as a bridge between two more treacherous rocks. Today, when the sun tipped over the trees and slid down the roof, today, where there had been no beach, fifty feet of gently sloping sand would reach to the angled shore break below.

They never minded when the sharp teeth of the coral reef were exposed. Reaching the waves became a game played between him and Jess – who could negotiate the rock road with the greatest speed and reach the beach first. It wasn't a matter of racing headlong over slippery rocks but more a game of skill and balance. Having spent more than half his life walking a tightwire, Jonah had a bit of an edge over Jess who only now, at nine-years-old, was learning to juggle. He found it easy to land like a dragonfly on a coral knuckle, catch his balance and know within seconds where he would fly next. He never slowed down, never hung back, never tried to tell Jess what to do. He knew that her eyes would follow him, her hands would swing out in imitation of his. She needed to feel her body move fluidly in space. There was no right or wrong way to fly.

More than once, Jonah had regretted his decision to let Jessica come here to this island so far from the coasts and live with her grandmother, but after the accident, he was too distracted to both care for Jessica and continue to perform daily. He knew clearly that she would have a marvelous life living here at the beach, but slowly, as slowly as the lizards that crept sluggishly down the wall at midday, she was disconnecting from her circus family, a community that nurtures and supports him and where she had spent the first five years of her life.

Circus life was lively, noisy, communal, but here on this rugged island Greta's mother's house stood alone, far from town, looking out to sea with only seagulls and sea creatures for neighbors. Jess spent most of her waking hours reading and talking to her grandmother about fishing. Up until last month, he feared she was beginning to share her grandmother's opinion of him, which wasn't very complimentary. Then she began to juggle. Now, she could easily keep three balls in the air, sometimes four. The juggling was showing her more about balance than he was capable of explaining.

Greta's mother had blamed him for Greta's death and no matter how many times he tried to tell her that walking a tightrope had nothing to do with the flying trapeze, that Greta performed with a troupe and he was not part of that troupe, his mother-in-law would point her finger at him and say sternly, *You were her husband. You you YOU should have checked that net. I checked my husband's nets, and his life didn't depend on those fishnets. Your wife trusted her LIFE to those nets. YOU, her husband, you should have checked.*

When she barked those knife-edged words at him for the fifth time, Jonah struggled to maintain confidence in his own innocence. Even though he knew that Greta's fellow performers shouldered the weight of any responsibility for the net, after a while he could feel the heaviness of that accusation slide onto his back. Greta was his wife, the mother of their child. There was certainly no question he was responsible for her safety, but she was also a performer, skilled and independent. Her safety required that he respect her independence.

What if he *had* insisted on checking the net? Would she even allowed him to do so? Even if he had, would she still have torn through? She had built up enough speed for a double somersault but instead of curling into circles of air, she sped past Enrique, just beginning his descent into the catching position, and then hit the side net like Cezanne's "Woman Diving into Water," hands stretched beyond her head, head locked between her bare arms, feet tight together. Her body was an arrow slicing through knotted rope as if it were gauzy cotton cloth. What could have stopped her? It made no sense. If some muscle had cramped, if for some reason she knew she couldn't begin to curl her body, why didn't she allow herself to fall straight down, limbs loose, arms cushioning her head? Why had she continued to fly?

No one wanted to talk about it afterwards. Enrique had instantly dropped into the net below, exactly as Greta should have dropped. He bounced once, caught the edge of the net with his hands and swung himself down to the floor of the arena, with the speed of a wasp, the delicacy of a butterfly. He was at Greta's side before Jonah could leap over the juggling clubs stacked at the edge of the ring. It was Enrique who had gathered Greta into his arms, wiped the blood from her face, Enrique who steadied her wobbling head, Enrique who kissed her eyes. When he looked up and saw Jonah, his eyes filled with tears, and when Jonah squatted down, Enrique gently shifted Greta's weight to Jonah's knees. Together, they shielded Greta's body from the crowds behind them. Together they waited, each holding on to the other and to Greta. Enrique's hand rested on Jonah's shoulder, Jonah's hand around Enrique's waist. Greta's torso lay flat on Jonah's knees, her legs twisted near Enrique's feet.

They waited without speaking until six clowns in full costume arrived with a board long enough and wide enough to support Greta's body. One clown in costume but without makeup ran in with the yellow silk flag used in the spec, the final extravaganza announcing the end of the show. Another followed pedaling fast on an over-sized bicycle with two enormous red flags streaming behind. The one with the yellow flag on his shoulder ran full speed while a tiny Chihuahua dressed in a bright silver spangled jacket, a polka-dotted hat, and purple pants nipped at his heels. Meanwhile, the clown on the bicycle took off furiously in the opposite direction, blowing frantically on a silver police whistle. The band played a rousing march to accompany the wild clown chase that continued pell-mell as someone, Jonah now thinks it must have been TC, the magician, released at least two dozen doves dyed the colors of the rainbow to fly in slow swooping circles into the rafters. Those in the crowd who were not watching the wild clown chase focused on the birds, spiraling ever closer to the ceiling.

As eyes looked up at the magic of the rainbow birds, few watched Jonah roll Greta's body onto the board. Few saw Enrique cover her body up to her chin with blue silk, another flag, this one printed with a golden sun. Those who did see would swear later that Greta was alive when she left the arena, that they had seen her turn her head, seen her smile, seen her lift her arm in a gentle wave. After all, the ringmaster had announced in full voice that she would *live,* accidents happen, ladies and gentlemen, he had heard her say she was okay. *She will live,* he sang out, *she will live!*

Enrique, Jonah, the clowns, almost every other member of their circus family who had seen her fly into the floor knew she died when her head slammed into the concrete floor of the arena, but the crowd had come to witness magic. No one wanted to believe they had witnessed death. The children would remember the doves and the tiny sparkling dog who could leap with all four feet from the ground and turn somersaults midair. The family, his circus family, made sure of that.

Every year after the season ended, the family circus splintered into more tender groupings that drifted off to tiny houses or trailers with backyards large enough for both practice and orange trees, but when everyone else went south to Florida, Jonah flew as far west as he could, half-way into the Pacific, caught a boat to this remote island, and then walked the six miles out to the end of the island where Greta's mother had both her house and a little shack for drying fish.

No airplanes. No buses, and no bicycles.

He relaxed the minute he climbed from the boat onto the rocky shore. Jonah never minded the walk along the gravel road. He enjoyed being out in the air, away from blinding spotlights and the droning hum of the arena, and there were enough spreading trees to keep the sun from being absurdly hot. This close to the equator, days without shade could be unbearable, making practice hard. He had learned that these last few years, but he kept coming back. This island was Jess' home now, and he needed Jess as much as she needed him.

As he never carried a large pack, he always arrived humming. Traveling with nothing more than a change of clothes, he always had room in his pack for small gifts for Jess and her grandma. This year he brought Jess a set of professional juggling balls, packed inside his rigging -- a slack wire he could stretch over the narrow canyon some distance from the coast and all the spikes needed to secure it. He loved these four months with Jess, but he needed to stay in shape, keep on the wire. Walking those first miles helped him to slow his pace, arrive smiling. Even without the sun beating on his neck, if he wanted to avoid dehydration, he found he had to walk slowly, but he was certainly familiar with such a deliberate pace. After all, the best way to cross a tightwire was with such delicate deliberation. The six-mile walk gave him time to decompress, and midway he could rest in the leafy cave someone had carved out of the hau thicket at the edge of a crystal clear stream that trembled across an open field before falling as a waterfall to the sea below.

This year when he stepped into the courtyard of the tiny house and waved, Jess came running with her arms spread wide. He laughed, pleased to see Jess' eyes move from grey to green when he handed her the juggling balls and even more pleased when she said she had something to show him. Something special. He had glanced at Greta's mother, curious, but she just smiled, a gentle quiet smile that opened petals around her eyes. Neither would offer even the slightest hint about the big secret.

He even urged Greta's mother to take a second glass of the sherry he had carried for her all the way from Philadelphia, thinking the warm flush of sherry might convince her to tell the secret, but she would answer no questions. Instead, she told a small story about a tiny octopus Greta once found trapped in a deep pool far from the waves, how she had visited it daily, bringing with her small bait fish and sand crabs she collected down at the beach. She had been certain that the waves would come and gather this graceful dancer, but when the beach began to grow, she decided that she needed to rescue her Inky. She unscrewed the handle from the mop, emptied out the kitchen garbage can, and trekked across the sand to rescue the poor stranded octopus. When she came home, she said, with a very serious look on her face, that finally she understood mermaids.

The day Greta's mom told the story, Jess listened intently, her eyes moving quickly from her Grandma's weathered face to her father's smile. Later Jonah sat on the terrace for at least an hour after Jess and her Grandma had gone to bed, thinking about mermaids and remembering Greta's hair flowing behind her as she flew from the trapeze, her jeweled smile, her flashing opal eyes, triumphant after she completed a successful double somersault. She was swimming through space. If he closed his eyes, he saw the light sparking behind her as she stood with Enrique on the platform, their arms wrapped lightly around each other's waist. When he opened his eyes, he saw only the indigo sky and rafts of stars moving at a pace he could not follow. Finally, as the Southern Cross began to shift across the horizon, he had gone to bed under a blanket of anticipation, feeling both warm and light, grateful for distance and the stars.

The next day and the day after that and the day after that, he and Jess walked on the beach, trying to see how they could spring across the rocks, dance with the sea. He scratched lines in the sand and told Jess stories about her mother as they walked, knee deep in the surf, pausing expectantly after each story finished, thinking that Jess's great secret would burst forth in waves of words and smiles, but she just looked up and asked him to please tell more. And he did, but as they splashed in the shallows, dove into waves, he would often pause, let the silence grow long and full, hoping for Jess to show him her miraculous something.

Now, after last night's sea change, today felt somehow different. The music of the surf was no longer dominated by the oompahpah of the tuba; instead, the thrumming was of distant drums. Jonah knew he had been right about the waves and the coming of the sand. By dawn, the waves were indeed breaking further out. By mid-morning, white sand stretched far from the front of the house, covering all the exposed coral, all the rocks that he and Jess had skipped across for the past few weeks. Gentle but uniform waves were breaking further out on the reef, sliding silver onto the shore.

Jess stepped out onto terrace and slipped her hand into his. "Perfect," she whispered, pointing to the waves.

Jonah lifted his hand onto her shoulder. She had grown taller this last year and her lithe body was muscular and browned by the sun as if she, too, spent hours working out back on the circus lot. Juggling, he thought. Jess was watching his eyes.

"Time for the surprise!" she said. "Grandma, come on, we can go!"

She pulled a wicker chair off the terrace and walked it midway down the new beach, settled it into the fresh sand. "You sit here."

She bowed to Jonah and gestured with the same wide wave of her arm her mother would use when she was introduced as the mermaid of the air.

Of course, Jonah sat.

He had been waiting for days for this, the grand surprise. He sat, hands in his lap, staring as the waves swelled and swamped, keeping his back to the terrace, waiting for her entrance. As he half expected her to come running down the beach, juggling her brand-new balls along with her old, he was surprised when both Jess and her grandmother walked hand-in-hand out on to the sand, stood some feet in front of him before raising their hands in solemn ceremony above their heads.

"Ladies and Gentlemen, um, that is to say, *Gentleman*, now, to the accompaniment of the Rock and Rollers, the Magnificent Starr Sisters will now perform their Mermaid Tango." Jess enunciated each word in a loud yet distinctly solemn voice.

Then, they bowed deeply and ran into the fish-drying shed, both giggling like mad, and came out wearing bright green bathing suits, each carrying surfboards painted to look like glistening fishtails.

Without missing a beat they walked, step matching step, to the water and paddled out to the furthest break. Neither pulled ahead of the other and both turned on the wave at the same moment. As their boards reached the top of the wave, both stood at the same moment, each with one arm, their opposing arm, raised. He felt as if he were seeing double. Their movements were perfectly synchronized. They could be as easily be on the flying trapeze as surfing these gentle and careful waves. The boards scooped up, then down, and each time they found the crest again, they also found a new position of balance on their boards. They dropped to one knee, lifted first their right leg, then their left. Finally, just as the wave neared shore, they shifted their boards into close parallel and came to shore holding hands and laughing.

"The dance Greta learned from the octopus," Grandma Starr said.

"The dance of the mermaid," Jess said.

The dance of love, Jonah thought, and blew them both a kiss.

Tomorrow, he would stretch his tight wire between the two breadfruit trees close to shore, dance just a little while watching Jess and her grandma moving in perfect parallel.

Life in balance.

Cloudbreak

Huge waves breaking on the beach before dawn. Fifteen-footers hitting the sand with a resounding thud and spraying back to the sky in a wild rush of lacy foam. Hearing the rhythm of the waves change to a spaceless roar, Blake and I had ventured out before dawn to walk the length of the beach, and now we were watching the great lolling tongues of water slide all the way to the naupaka far from the shore break. We chattered on about the weatherman on Hawai`i's "Severe Weather Station" who's been shrieking for days about 40-footers coming soon to the north shore and twenty footers on the west. And here we were standing on the western shore, and there they were, twenty footers. Right in front of us.

We never really paid too much mind to the dour announcements of impending doom on the "Severe Weather Station". After all, why in the world would Hawai`i, where gentle trade winds blow almost continually and temperatures hover around 80 year round, need a "severe" weather station? Who thought that one up? Laughing, we stand facing the sea and open wide our arms to the rumbling waves. What they thought apocalyptic, we thought grand.

Of course, in Makaha, no one is expecting any forty-foot waves, but even in this low light, I can see the waves breaking out past the point are far larger than twenty feet. Even the shore break is considerably taller than my six-feet-two even after their silky stone faces collapse to foam. Before these waves dive fist-first onto the sand, the moon paints a glistening sheen on their faces that shimmers like the wet skin of some great serpent, but even that sea serpent can't stay intact. The minute the snake opens its mouth, it falls apart, rolling head over heels, teeth in the sand, leaving behind a gathered foam, liquid green but less like lace than like a glacier suddenly released from its icy cage, moving at a pace anything but glacial. The waves have that weight, that power.

I glance at Blake, tighten my gentle grasp of her elbow. She has been upright again for only a few days, and although this dawn walk was her idea, I am still a bit uncertain, worried about the unpredictability of the sea this morning. I know it must be hard for her to be so close to such waves and wonder if I have made a huge mistake bringing her here. Of course, I don't really know if this is hard for her or joyous. All I do know is when she turns her face to mine, she's smiling. Perhaps, she's remembering the rush of being on the lip of the wave before it tumbled her mercilessly into a shoreline unwilling to yield.

We're waiting for dawn, but the sun is slow this morning. It stays hidden behind the mountains as if not yet ready to risk shaking hands with this unruly visitor, this wild surging sea. When dawn finally does break, the crash and roll of the huge waves sprays fine droplets of salt water that linger on air, trapping sun first as red then green then a brilliant gold. The houses on the far side of the beach appear blurred and the few surfers floating on the waves are nothing more than charcoal smudges.

"Do you have the feeling we're walking in someone's pastel drawing?" Blake raises her arm to gesture towards the blurred palm trees beyond the apartment building.

"Well, if we are, that artist sure has a heavy hand. I never heard pastels make such a racket, even when brand-new." We both laughed.

After the accident, while waiting for her leg to heal, Blake had tried her to regain the use of her shattered arm by drawing. After the cast had come off her arm, she found that she only had limited use of her hand and determined to change that. She had asked me to staple large sheets of paper to the one living room wall approachable by wheelchair and had set up a small table where she laid out sharpened pencils, bits of charcoal, and arranged by color, lines of brand-new pastels her sister had sent from NYC. Easier to buy good pastels at Pearl Paint than at Long's, she said.

She also asked me to fashion a tool that would allow her to draw on the upper reaches of the stapled paper without leaving her wheelchair. I thought about it for days, imagining shiny stainless arms that I might fashion down at Keola's machine shop in the boatyard but then decided simple is best. I attached a clamp to a piece of bamboo that would allow her to grab and firmly hold a pastel. It would serve basically as an extension of her arm, but she would have to lock her fingers about its smooth green surface. Better to exercise her finger muscles. If she wanted to paint again, she needed to regain fine motor control.

At first, the bamboo tool had lain on the table unused. She could barely lift her arm. It was all she could do to get her fingers to hold the pastel and her hand to make short vertical strokes at the bottom of the paper closest to the wheelchair. The first drawings looked like some sort of weird oasis, a closely cropped patch of rainbow colored grass in the middle of a white sand desert beneath a glaring African sky.

Having known so intimately her lush abstracts that seemed to morph unreasonably from breathtaking sunsets to overheated body interiors, I felt my heart contract every time I looked at those short stabbed lines isolated by vast reaches of white space to either side and well above. To create those tiny densely packed rectangles of rainbow colored lines exhausted her and swallowed every waking hour up until mid-afternoon.

Blake avoided lunch and drew for as many hours before noon as she could and maybe two following. Her showdown at the OK Corral, she called it, or slowdown, she would sometimes add. After relaxing her grip on the last pastel in her "line-up," she slept deeply, and I watched the determined mask she wore while struggling to lift her arm to mark the paper finally relax to the warm radiance that had been the only make-up she needed before she had smashed into the Makaha sands two years ago.

Too many nights, too many days, too many hours, I've wasted asking "what if." What if we had gone instead to the Riviera? What if we had never come out to Makaha? It had been so very many years since Blake had been surfing, after all. But she had wanted desperately to go to Makaha, her beloved Makaha, and I could never refuse Blake. After the unexpected success of Blake's London show, I had asked her what she wanted to do to celebrate.

Oh, Keith, she said, I *want to go home. I want to swim again in the swelling seas of Makaha, offer thanks to the ocean. Don't you see, Keith? The ocean gave me these paintings. These are tidal tunnels.*

Tidal tunnels.

I had to think about that but not for long. Blake frequently had "poetic" things to say about her paintings and none of them made much sense to me. I could have challenged her on the tidal tunnels thing, but I knew from past experience I would get nowhere. I could have said, Come on, Blake, everyone knows that tides in Hawai`i are measured by inches not by feet and how in the world can such casual tides create tunnels.

I could've said that but didn't.

When we first met, I had tried to show her tides, real tides, tides measured by feet not inches, and double-digit feet at that. We drove for hours from Boston to downeast Maine to meet my folks up there, me chattering on about lobster traps, she fiddling incessantly with the radio dial, looking for jazz stations. I knew she loved the ocean so I told her about the wild currents of Passamaquoddy Bay, promised to show her something that would positively blow her mind. Blake never liked surprises so she tried her hardest to get me to spill the beans during the long ride up the coast, but I just smiled and told her about my Aunt Ruth's luncheonette and my Dad's fishing shack down near the shore.

It was dark by the time we arrived in Eastport and as usual the town was shuttered. Even the Dunkin' Donuts was locked up tight. We drove through town to the "shack," really a miniature two story house complete with a fireplace and a tiny tiny bathroom that Dad had installed in what had used to be the storeroom for nets and such when Mom told him she wasn't going to set foot in that camp again if she had to pee in a bucket. When Dad said something about the "great outdoors," I could've sworn I heard Mom growl.

If Dad hadn't been so in love with Mom, her thick black hair that hung to her waist, her flashing smile, and especially her fiddle playing, he might have shrugged and said *Suit yourself,* and then used the camp as so many men use such rickety buildings in desolate places – as a place to escape, if ever so briefly, from the strictures of marriage, but Dad never wanted to escape marriage. He was a man in love, a man who loved, and Mom felt the same about him. They were a sight to see, sitting in the late afternoon in their postage stamp back yard, Mom with her fiddle tucked under her chin and Dad just listening with this goofy look on his face as she shifted from the "Louisiana Hornpipe" to Bach's "Partita #1 in B Minor". He never got tired of listening to her play and she never got tired of playing. Music, he once said in one of those exceedingly uncomfortable father-to-son puberty talks, was better than sex.

I wasn't sure I believed him then and I'm not sure I believe him now, but when that great wave finally gasped and spit Blake's twisted body on to shore, I did think about what my Dad had said that rainy afternoon when we sat for so long looking at the Bay, talking of this and that. Then, after the doctors finished putting Blake back together, after they told me soberly that it would take a while but that she would live, she would walk again, I made my way as fast as I could to her hospital room carrying a portable CD player and a shopping bag filled with jazz CDs – Miles Davis, Oscar Peterson, Thelonius Monk, Nina Simone, Coltrane, Stephane Grapelli.

Mom used to love to play "Honeysuckle Rose" in early summer when her double pink climbing rose was in full bloom, and "Anything Goes" was one of her standards, maybe even her signature song. After playing for hours, even if she had been playing Schubert, she would play that song in the style of Grapelli and then collapse laughing on the couch next to my Dad. He would smile a smile would melt all winter ice from windows and put his arms around her as if she were the most tender and most beautiful flower on earth.

I wasn't about to lose Blake. I wanted her music to mingle with mine. I remembered what my Dad had said about music.

That weekend in Eastport, Mom and Dad didn't arrive until afternoon, which gave me some time to introduce Blake to the town. The very first thing I introduced her to was the tide. As usual, I woke before she did and put the kettle onto boil water for coffee – no Mr. Coffee here – and by the time I had set the tiny table on the porch with steaming mugs and the fresh blueberry muffins I'd picked up before leaving Boston, the waters of the bay were beginning their daily departure. By evening, we would be again looking at fleets of fishing boats, bobbing about on a sparkling blue bay, but this morning very soon the view from the porch would one of mud flats, littered with trash thrown off the pier and out of portholes. Blake stepped onto the porch just as the retreating water was beginning to gather speed. She rubbed her eyes and then gasped.

Keith! She shrieked, gesturing frantically towards the bay. *We have to get out here.*

I, of course, just uncovered the jam jar and pushed the cream pitcher in her direction.

No really. Look, Keith, look!

Just as I was about to explain about the tide when she burst out, *The waters are receding! Tidal Wave! Tsunami coming! Tsunami!*

Of course, I laughed and, of course, she refused to speak to me for the rest of the day and made sure she told my Mom and Dad about my "joke" again and again until finally by evening when the waters rushed back like horizontal waterfalls, she was laughing, too. Perhaps Blake's paintings were tidal tunnels after all, undersea washes where mermaids sat and combed their hair. It made sense somehow that she would be painting edgeless landscapes without discernible form. No seaweed bushes. No seahorse trees. Just the weight of rhythm tunneled beneath the waves. Somewhere in all that blue, violins.

"Look."

Blake had stopped. I could feel her weight resting heavily on my arm. I knew we wouldn't walk any further this morning, but somehow that didn't matter. We were on the beach beside waves. Huge waves, waves that landed on the surfing beach with a resounding thud that shook the beach, and Blake was smiling. Despite the weight of her body, I could detect no fear in her touch. She sucked her breath in and touched my arm. The tips of her fingers felt electric. "Look, Keith."

Out beyond the point, a huge wave was rising. I had never seen waves like this in the Atlantic. Had we still been draped by pre-dawn shadows, that wave might have looked opaque, as dense as a fin of a shark large enough to swallow the entire island whole, but because the sun was now slanting on the sea, the deeper blue of deeper waters thinned rapidly to a transparent turquoise as the wave rose. Pure white lace fringed the perfect curve of the wave that seemed to pull ever higher towards the sky until suddenly the delicate white lace became a waterfall rushing over some unseen cliff, home, I'm sure, to sharp-beaked birds with wings wider than history. I leaned down and let my lips brush Blake's eyes.

"Tidal tunnels," I said.

"Astronomical tides," she replied, and suddenly I understood. The tidal tunnels Blake painted weren't undersea. She was finding her way through tunnels to the stars above, zooming out past the moon.

Regreso

The last of May and bitter cold.

Ella pulled the lapels of her thin wool coat even tighter across her chest, but still the winds blustered through the fabric, biting at bones exposed by months of living without without fat or sugar. A diet of eggplant, rice and tomatoes drops pounds faster than any suavely concocted diet neatly meted out by well-coifed white-shirted "technicians" at that fancy spa her Aunt Bertha used to insist she frequent as a "cure" for her jumpy nerves. Six months in Africa had worked better than that mint-green placidly neutral zone of Vivaldi, hot water, and mint facials. She now knows that the dry blasting winds of harmattan, smoke from eternal trash fires, men with machine guns, unending heat and dribs and drabs of food kill all nerves, jumpy or not. The fact that this morning she felt anything at all was somehow hopeful. Bring on the cold.

The boats in the harbor were bobbing at odd angles as the wind sliced across the grey waters. On other mornings, when the sun was shining, sea birds swooped and dived as white sails slid easily in front of the hulking tankers chugging out of port. Then, Ella stood with her back to the city and sang, her voice the only wind touching the backs of the birds. She kicked the curb and screwed her eyes shut. "May doesn't deserve to be this cold. I don't deserve to be this cold."

"Leas' you gotta coat, girl. I ain't got no coat."

Ella turned quickly. She hadn't realized she had spoken aloud. Nearby, a wiry woman leaned into the wind, her bare feet rooted to the rotting boards of the pier, bare arms like peeled sticks inches above the blue-painted steel railings.

Ella began peeling off her own coat. "Please."

"Ah, sheez, hon, ain't so bad as all tha'. Really, keep ya coat." The woman brushed her grey hair from her face and grinned a gap-toothed smile. "I ain't no spring chicken. I know cold worsen dis. How can I be cold with all dis here?"

She swept her hand in a slow arc above her head and her fingertips seemed to touch the wings of the few birds that were flying determinedly on top of the wind. When her hand dropped, she reached into one of the many bags piled beside her and pulled out a tiny white paper sack.

"Heah, hav' some peanut. Peanut alway make ya feel bettah."

Despite the cold, cheerful spring flowers bloomed in wild rushes of red and gold with spasmodic outbursts of purple, hothouse grown but now at home in the redwood planting boxes nestled against the benches facing the harbor waves. She was sure that there would be days when the sun would no longer be a pale arctic stream, days when she might sit with her legs stretched to those blue railings, her feet catching the cooling spray of passing boats. Clearly, the cold was temporary, a quirk of spring, a bit of north blowing down the coast from Alaska, the last of winter. The flowers were proof of warmer days, past and future.

She recalled few flowers blooming under the white-hot sun of Yola, but there were some. A few almost invisible blue flowers hugged the ground by her front door, bravely opening every dawn. By noon, they melted into the blue gray mat of dusty leaves that spread listlessly across the sand. She couldn't gather them, but nonetheless she had been grateful they were there. Often, despite her exhaustion, she had found herself waking at dawn, just so she might see those blue petals unfold. On days when the sun was blood red and huge on the horizon, days when she knew by noon it would be too hot to breathe, she'd wanted to prostrate herself before those cobalt gems scattered on the ground, offer solemn prayers to their naked beauty.

"Come on, hon, hav' a peanut. Do ya sum good."

The woman stretched her hand, palm up, fingers cupped, jiggling the red-skin nuts ever so slightly.

Ella recoiled as she smelled the rancid nuts piled there. Ella hated peanuts. Groundnuts, they called them in Yola. Groundnuts and goat, groundnuts and radish, groundnuts and eggplant. Major food. Unfortunately, groundnuts grow in the *ground* and the earth where the peanuts grew teemed with parasites, little beasties that if swallowed settled happily into the miles of intestines stuffed below the stomach where they would live like teenagers, tossing their trash here there and everywhere. All that trash did the same thing to the interior body landscape as trash does to any landscape. Drains clogged, interesting and more productive flora died unceremoniously, and before long, the interior landscape began to look pretty bleak. Nothing grew, evil gasses spiraled up from the clogged drains, escaping at all the wrong moments.

Peanuts. No way to clean them in Yola. Potatoes, carrots, radishes, they could be cleaned. For some reason, soaking potatoes in that lovely 'sterilizing' fluid called 'Milton' always worked. So cool that Milton eradicated parasites. Somehow Ella always knew that about Milton. Book Five of *Paradise Lost* taught her Milton could eradicate any evil he chose to erase.

'Milton' as magic.

Use 'Milton' and potatoes get clean, but soak groundnuts in 'Milton,' and the little parasitic beasties just burrow deeper into peanut flesh. Okay, coating peanuts in salt works, but cupfuls of salt together with dead parasites is not exactly appetizing. No thanks. Ella gave up eating groundnuts her second week in Yola, about the same time she gave up on eggs and chicken, and now, she's not about to go back to crunching down on parasites, real or imagined. Of course, these peanuts are no doubt grown in pristine soils but just looking at them, Ella could see crowds of electric green bugs, each with several overgrown heads and more legs than made sense. She saw no reason to allow fresh populations of mutant bugs to join the now dying crowds in her lower intestines who had been having such fun chowing down on the last bits of fat on her thighs. She's just a bit tired of their fisticuffs.

Ella looked around, first to her left, then to her right. The old woman with the threadbare clothes had gone, vanished into the fog. Or so it seemed. No more peanuts. No more bugs with green eyes and yellow heads, but still plenty of wind. Disappearance happens in more ways than expected. First, memories go and then the world. The remains, bits and pieces of worlds belonging to others, seem inconsequential, so unnecessary and absurd.

On the days when she sings, the world stays alive. The music matters, but on the days when the song is drowned by fog and wind, even the black crowned night heron standing on one leg at the end of the pier looks like a Museum of Natural History display, wings permanently glued to his side, head beneath his wing. It doesn't matter where the old woman went, just that she went and went cold. She had no coat. Ella's own coat was still draped over her arm. An old kindly mother who had offered her sustenance faded into the fog, coatless. Not right.

Ella's own mother had been a singer, practicing all afternoon and singing all night in jazz clubs, belting out stripped down songs about sharks with pearly teeth, stormy weather, and stars falling on Alabama. After she died, Ella went to Africa, wanting distance from the Louisiana bayou, black freighters, and pounding pianos. She had convinced herself that in Africa music would be attached to stones and knife-edge skies. She had been wrong, of course. Not dead wrong, fortunately, but wrong enough.

All she'd found were bleak landscapes covered with piles and piles of trash and piles and piles of ash once the trash burned, all mixed up by a too hot sun. She stopped singing altogether. No one had been interested in her sea chanteys, out of place and out of time in that blistering desert. She had thought that she would find her mother's music there, and then find a way into the more erratic rhythms of scat, but the only scat she found was underfoot and sea music, attached to her bones, was as foreign there as she was.

For years, she had been angry at her mother for naming her Ella, a name that have given no end of trouble when she had been studying medieval music in Boston. Ella? Folks would say, like Ella Fitzgerald, and she would nod, explain that her mother was a jazz singer playing the clubs on the fringes of New Orleans and she herself was studying voice.

Instantly she would be invited to this party or that, expected to entertain with jazzy renditions of "Misty" or "Between the Devil and the Deep Blue Sea." She tired of explaining that just because she was black and just because her name was Ella didn't mean she could sing those songs. Even though her skin was dark she was also fifty percent Irish, and, by the way, she would rather sing "The Mermaid," did they know it? Of course, they never did, and inevitably some yahoo would make some remark about the "Black Irish," and she would know that the time had come for her to look for her coat and go home. After a while, she learned to politely decline those party invitations that followed conversations that had included explanations of her name and then learned to avoid any mention at all of her singing career in casual conversation.

Ella's mother had met her father when she was entertaining the troops in London during the last days of World War II, and they had had a whirlwind courtship, marrying only ten days after they met, but the marriage had lasted. Her red-haired blue-eyed father had adored her mother until the day he died, and her mahogany skinned mother had never stopped loving him even after he died. When she was young, long before he grew so sick and died, her father would grab hold of any opportunity to tell the story of how he had been enchanted by this young singer as beautiful as any woman he had ever seen but, oh no, he would say, that wasn't why he fell in so deep in love he could barely speak.

It was her voice, he said. He was sure Ella Fitzgerald had never sang "It Ain't Necessarily So" with the same sly humor and below the belt passion as did his lovely Merrilee. Then or now. When she hit that first "Wadoo, zim bam boddle-oo, hoodle ah da wa da," he near about fainted, and when the chorus came round a second time, he decided. She had cast her spell.

He was going to marry that gal.

At that juncture of the story, Ella's mother would always chime in and let her voice be heard, singing the final verse about Methuselah living for nine hundred years, but who calls that living when no gal will give in to no man's what's nine hundred years, and then while laughing so hard she could barely breathe, she'd pick up the story line, explain how this skinny ass sailor with skin so white she thought he musta been bleached or wrapped in a sheet had 'appeared' (yeah, he musta been some kinda ghost) up at the stage door with pink roses taped to his crutches and one bright red rose still a bud between his teeth. She'd laughed and laughed at the sight of that ole bony ghost, but oh my, there was something about those blue blue eyes, she said, something about that sea sparkle, something about his shy *kind* smile, that made her say yes when he asked her to dinner the following night and something about those pale musical hands, almost like water, that made her say yes every night after that. She was enchanted, she guessed, enchanted by his fire hair, his down-to-earth smile, his sea eyes, his transparent hands. Nothing forced about your father, she said. He was genuine, the real McCoy. He was kind and still is, she said, still is.

After the war, they settled outside of New Orleans. Her mother reconnected with the club owners she had known before she went overseas, and her father bought an old shrimp boat, painted it green, took to the waves, came back daily with pounds and pounds of fish and shrimp. Ella's parents were lively, magical and funny, but that was no excuse for naming her Ella. Ella shook her head but didn't scowl. She had to laugh. She missed them, but really, it *was* unfair, especially as they had never really wanted her to sing like Ella anyway.

Once, when she was fourteen, she had practiced in secret "It Ain't Necessarily So" until she thought she had it *down,* and then rearranged the living room to look like a club, set a bottle of wine on a tiny wrought iron table between two comfortable chairs and invited her folks in for "cocktails." They had come not knowing what to expect and she had entertained them just as those curious about her name later hoped to be entertained and never were. She couldn't help notice that her father looked decidedly uneasy as she trilled her way through that first "Wadoo zim bam boddle-oo" and couldn't understand why her mother had that strained look on her face. After the final note, her father applauded politely and her mother cleared her throat, getting ready, Ella thought, to offer well-meaning advice, but Ella never gave her the chance. Not ready for critical appraisal, she turned around twice, hoping they would not see her rain eyes, smiled brightly and returned to the piano. This time she played "The Mermaid," singing through seawinds and around the corner of desperate cliffs. She watched the glazed scrim lift from her father's eyes and her mother's face open as a rose opens to the first real summer sun. After that, she sang only the bright glass of sea chanteys.

Now, even as the sun rose above the tops of the office buildings, bouncing daggers of gold light from windows, the wind danced a steady pace. The surface of the bay was overwhelmed by sharp white caps that lifted and fell in a rhythm more like steel than music. The wind was still cold, and Ella had to admit to herself that even with the sun, it might not get any warmer before noon. If she wanted warmth she had to head for the café at the edge of the waterfront park, sit, and drink tea. She glanced at her watch. 9 a.m. The café would be open.

At this hour and in this wind, few wandered about the park and fewer still were sitting scattered about the café, hunkered over steaming cups of coffee. Ella soon had a tall cup of tea and a cinnamon apple scone (another thing she had missed in Africa – pastries) and settled onto the couch nearest the window to sip her tea and read. Just to be ornery, she was reading a 13th century Chinese text that had been translated in the 19th century by some dry academic who obviously felt that no translation could possibly be any good unless it was absolutely literal, which made for tough reading, but she was slogging through. Finally, she had to admit that the book bored her. She closed it carefully and began to listen to room about her.

The hiss of milk steaming into hot coffee. Nina Simone singing "Please, Don't Let Me Be Misunderstood." The casual chatter of a young couple, trying to decide which movie to see later in the day. The clatter of spoons, and the cheerful banter of the coffee server. He was laughing, and the distinct lilting accent of that laugh made her smile. Suddenly, she realized as she listened to him call out completed orders that his accent was both familiar and distinctly out of place in this café with its glass display cases overflowing with croissants, scones, and muffins big enough to feed an entire family. Ella picked up her book and walked to the counter.

Looking at the cheerful young man, she asked a question that she hoped was not impolite or impolitic. "Are you from Nigeria?"

He stopped, set his hand on the counter, and smiled a broad smile. "Hoo, girl, you understand language. Yeah. Lagos."

"Hmm," Ella twisted her eyebrows. "Your accent sounds more like Northern Nigeria than Lagos."

"Hoo, girl, you're *real* good. Yeah, I grew up in Kano." He was looking at her with greater interest now.

"I just returned from Nigeria."

"Ahhhh," he paused, turned and picked up a large white mug from the shelf behind him, selected a pyramidal tea bag from the glass jar near the cash register, "Where were you?"

"Yola."

The minute the name left her lips and landed on the counter, he was laughing. He laughed and laughed in that rich full way that Nigerians have of laughing. He laughed until the whole room was blooming with his laughter, until everyone had abandoned their newspapers and their cups to turn their heads and look.

"Yola." He thrust his hand across the counter and shook her hand, pumped it up then down, up then down, again and again. "Yola. Well, girl, all I can say is congratulations, you got out. You made it. Hot there, isn't it? Hot. Too hot to breathe. You got out."

"Yeah," Ella said, "Yeah, I got out." She smiled. It had been hot all right, thick air, dust, 118 degrees Fahrenheit every day, but she didn't say that.

She just said, "Yeah, hot. Too hot to breathe." She knew he understood.

His grin grew until it seems as if his face crack, and then shaking his head ever so slightly from side to side as if amazed or bemused, he repeated himself just as she had repeated him.

"Too hot to breathe. Yeah. You got out."

He shook his head again, this time slower and wider, waving his hand in front of his eyes, and like magic, the slow arc of his arms crossing in front of his face replaced the shining stainless steel restaurant equipment with visions of dusty shelves empty except for dented sardine cans and empty water bottles. The returning wave of his arms replaced the bodies of early morning coffee drinkers calmly reading he morning news with visions of soldiers masked behind dark glasses, machine guns tight to their chests.

He looked at Ella; she looked back at him. They both wanted to say more, but that gesture, that wave of arms, hands floating across eyes, would have to be it. Beside her, a young man with blond dreadlocks had begun to drum his fingers on the counter. Narrowing his eyes, he opened his mouth, readied himself for speech, but before he could say a word, the counterman from Kano, turned to him.

"Yes, young man, and how may I serve you?"

Whistlestop

With dawn came the hollow whistle of freight trains, slowing as they chugged through downtown, passing the once bustling department stores and the high-rise condo buildings minus doormen but still nattily dressed with brightly painted "For Rent" signs. At this hour, the streets were relatively empty. A few stray dogs as skinny as dust ducked in and out of alleys, sometimes emerging with greasy bits of paper or a half-chewed sandwich, and then, if another dog approached, there would be a scuffle, an explosion of dirt and fur.

Even though it was not bitterly cold – no snow, no ice – Eduardo blew on his hands and stamped his feet. He shifted from foot to foot and glanced again at the cluster of office buildings to the east. At another time of year, the sun would already be snapping smartly between the sharp corners of the buildings, glancing bits of tinseled rainbows off window panes while bathing the courtyard in warm or perhaps even too hot floods of sun, but now, in December, the sun stayed locked behind brick, making a brief appearance only for the lunchtime crowd who never seemed to want to venture far from doorways. It seemed easier and more desirable to stay close to walls. After all, the heavy winter sky might fall at any minute.

Today, the open courtyard seemed too vacant, too chilly for casual strolling. No room for lounging on grey concrete benches. No resting between the downdrafts of dreary fog. All the flirtatious finger flicks of summer had been packed away beneath jackets and leather gloves. All open minds stuffed beneath woolen caps. All warm hearts hidden behind gripped lapels, dragging scarves. But not all was grey and dreary. 'Twas the season. Red ribbons of doors. Cheery wreaths hung behind plate glass, but even the holiday trees with their tiny white twinkling lights wrapping every bare branch looked miserable and cold. The season to be jolly. Ho ho ho.

At this time of year, Eduardo often wondered why he had come to this hard-edged city with its cold fogs and cracked sidewalks, but this year he wondered why he stayed. Three years ago when he first arrived, he had come downtown dressed in his neatly pressed suit, resumé in hand, confident that he would find the same work he had enjoyed in Mexico but with better pay. He had been confident he might easily find a job. Who wouldn't want to hire a bilingual talented salesman with an advanced degree in Comparative Religions from the Universidad Nacional Autónoma de México?

He was alert, open-minded, and ready to work. He was a better than adequate writer, well-organized and always cheerful on the job. He knew he had what it takes to succeed, but after three months of pushing his resumé across newly polished desks of executive secretaries with lacquered hair and dull smiles, he had grown discouraged. His easy smile had become as grey and as artificial as those of the young women who accepted his resumé, offering no encouragement other than the repetitive obviously memorized message *We'll call you if something opens up*, delivered in a flat dry monotone that seemed almost mechanistic. Their voices were definitely metallic but more like pitted pot metal than polished steel.

He remembered one day when he was tempted to brush his fingers on the arm of one woman who reached to accept his resumé. Not because she attracted him, but simply because he needed to know if she were indeed flesh, blood, and bones. He had begun to suspect that all these receptionists and secretaries were actually manufactured elsewhere of cheap tin. In China? In Mexico? Maybe even in his Uncle's factory, snapped together by machines before being shipped here as robot guard dogs, programmed only to bark out one sentence – the same sentence – every time. On that day, he resisted the impulse to touch the secretary's skin and pushed the elevator button instead. When he left the building, he stood for quite some time in the sun on this very same corner, feeling its warmth travel his face, letting his own thumb circle the tiny scar on the palm of his left hand. His flesh felt dry yet nourished somehow.

He could hear blood grumbling in his temples. He was real. The rest? He wasn't sure.

The very next day, Eduardo had brushed the lint from his suit, hung it carefully in a dry-cleaner bag borrowed from his cousin Luis, and then went downtown to the Goodwill to buy himself a pair of sturdy boots and two pairs of barely worn jeans. One pair was brand-new, and those he washed several times to make them appear well-used, and then, for the next two weeks he went every day to the ghetto to wait along with dozens of other men in the day-hire zone.

On the second day, a man driving a red BMW had asked him in broken Spanish if he could plaster walls, and he had nodded vigorously, murmuring "Si, si, si, señor" even though he had not a clue how to mix or apply plaster. By noon, he learned that plaster had a life of its own. His earlier idea of just adding water to the powder, mixing to a reasonable consistency, and then smearing it over holes and cracks was an idea not a practical solution. Then, using perfect English, he explained to the foreman that really he knew nothing about plaster but if there was any work in the office, he would be more than happy to oblige, that he was a fair typist, had a good grasp of numbers, understood the art of letter writing and had no trouble spelling even the most obscure English words.

The foreman then explained in perfect Spanish to two burly men lustily hoisting sheetrock from the truck that they should escort the "gentleman" from the construction site, which they did, using no words, Spanish or English. Each grabbed one arm and dragged him out the gate, heaving him without ceremony into the street.

After that little fiasco, Eduardo only spoke English to potential employers, trying very hard to sound willing and ready to work, smart but not necessarily educated. He learned to speak in small clear sentences, using only the simplest words, pausing every now and again to insert a series of stuttered uh-uh-uhs. When he got really good at that, he tried peppering his sentences with a "you know" or two. After all, potential bosses liked to think they knew a thing or two. This strategy landed him a few jobs, including one walking dogs, a job that was good only for one day. He never had much of a rapport with dogs and when the well-coifed standard poodle lifted his leg and water-stained his new jeans, he politely told the young men who had hired him that he would not return but thank you very much and please give a big hug to Bobo.

On his next job, he worked with six men far more burly and much more determined than he, clearing trash from an abandoned house. The stench was unbearable; several times he had to rush for the front door to keep from adding decorative elements to the walls that would, no doubt, smell as bad and be as hard to clean as that which they scraped from the floors. He was fired, told he didn't work fast enough, but again, he was not too sorry to lose the job.

After that, he spent one very long day caring for a cute and, as it turned out, very demanding ten-month old baby. At the end of the day he was exhausted and embarrassed by his own ignorance of babies. Like the plastering, he had thought such work would be easy. After all, he had once been a baby and he remembered his youngest brother mewling happily while his grandmamma cooed and jiggled him on her knee. He tried doing that with this rosy-cheeked babe, but instead of mewling, the baby cried and cried. He offered him a bit of his sandwich, which he refused, a sip of his water, which he accepted, but still the baby cried and cried. When the mother called late in the afternoon and heard the wild wails of her baby, she hung up on him.

He had been afraid something had happened to her, but moments later he heard her burst through the door. She flung her coat on the couch and gathered the poor babe up without saying one word to him but with many soft hums and coos to the baby, who drew many sharp hiccups as she exhaled vowels before both settled into a back and forth of gentle humming chords. When the young mother opened the refrigerator and saw the bottle of milk and the jars of strained plum still sitting on the shelf, she turned and looked at Eduardo with stony eyes. Her mouth opened, but no words would come out. She breathed deeply, hugged her baby tighter, and then pointed, rather desperately he thought, at the door. Needless to say, she never paid him the seven dollars an hour she had promised him. There were other missteps. Imagining reality didn't really work out so well. Sometimes work required real experience.

Eduardo leaned heavily into the brick, shifted his feet, flexed his fingers, and unbuttoned his coat. The day was warming ever so slightly. There had to be sun somewhere – above the clouds, away from the buildings, on the other side of the railroad tracks. Suddenly, the air felt soft, almost pliable, as if it should smell of apricots instead of grease. Indeed, if he breathed, he tasted the blue distance of train whistles mixed inexplicably with a delicacy that didn't exist on this street corner, the sweet honey of the roses blooming on the bush in his Tia's yard, roses that had been planted by his grandfather's grandfather too many years ago to count.

What roses they were! Single blooms, deep yellow that paled to white. Their abundance covered the blue-painted wall at the back of the garden very near the great bushes of basil and the creeping mats of thyme. He had spent many afternoons curled on a low cedar bench near the fountain, reading and waiting for the afternoon winds to blow a flurry of petals across his cheeks. He had read all of Cervantes, Lorca, and then got lost in the pages of Gabriel Garcia Marquez. If this morning he tasted roses, on those other mornings, he had tasted jungles with vines that erupted past parrots.

"Life." Eduardo inhaled deeply and slowly exhaled.

"Life is beautiful."

A young woman sitting near the dry fountain looked up, startled by Eduardo's sudden exclamation. She brushed her hand across her forehead and dropped her magazine. Her bare arm was lightning against the sky. He laughed loudly as she turned slowly, staring in his direction. He had spoken to no one in particular. He hadn't even realized that he had spoken aloud, but her eyes flashed and her body stiffened as if she had been attacked.

"Is it not? Is not life beautiful? It is, it is." Eduardo bowed deeply in her direction, his head almost scraping the pavement, hoping to show her he meant no harm. He pulled his arms from his overcoat and held his own bare arms overhead. The sun washed over his skin with a warmth that felt like his mother's breath as she leaned to kiss him good night when he was small and afraid of the dark.

"Look at those clouds moving across the sky. They dance. Look at the birds, the patternmakers, the dancers. Tell me that is not beautiful!"

Eduardo swept his hands in broad circles above his head. Then, the girl shifted her weight off one hip and onto her feet. Unsettled by this sudden explosion of joy, she was ready to scuttle away. She glanced about nervously, her fingers spread, balanced beside her like spiders. Happiness was not an everyday occurrence in this drab courtyard.

Eduardo danced lightly into the center of the courtyard and leaped atop the concrete bench, tipping his face to meet the passing clouds. He dropped his coat and hat on the bench beside him and flung his arms out. The girl hurriedly retrieved her magazine and was gathering her papers when Eduardo began to sing in a tenor voice as delicate as the first ice edging a stream but as rich as the mud that ran beneath. He sang boldly and freely, not just any song but Alfredo's passionate aria about the dream of shared life, a wonderful life, ecstatic life, *De miei bollenti spiriti* from *La Traviata*.

His voice had a roughness that was interesting rather than disturbing. Consonants cut through the air and vowels piled into invisible cushions on the concrete. Something, something critical, was not shared but that which was not shared was as important as that which was. As his voice soared upward, that something unsaid, that something unsung trembled behind, and the taut friction between the two settled upon the sidewalk like lace on an old weathered cactus. The spine of that which lay beneath was instantly visible, isolated enough as to glow in the sun while that which settled delicately on top – the lace – was somehow fresher and more exquisite because the rough spines beneath were exposed to air and sun.

The timid girl at the fountain moved off, scurrying away at unreasonable speed, dragging her long purple overcoat behind her, but others arrived to listen. Those who had been crossing the courtyard on their way back to work stopped cold. Those who had been waiting at street corners for lights to change, changed direction and walked to within four feet of Eduardo. Soon the courtyard was filled with people, some glancing furtively and questioningly at one another, but some smiling quietly while others looked boldly at Eduardo.

Before he could take a breath, folks began to drop coins into his hat and then dollar bills, but Eduardo didn't notice as the dollar bills became five-dollar bills, then tens and twenties. He wasn't singing to them or for them. He was singing because that was the only thing to do on a day when the sun remained low in the sky and the fog threatened to return too soon. He was singing because the sky was open, because the rose in his heart was blooming, because winter no longer felt cold. Because it was the season.

January Tides

The cove outside was bumping about like so many rats caught in an unexpected snowstorm, surging upwards as if in search of a known but yet undiscovered opening to warmth. No longer smoothed by summer winds, the waves were chopped to tiny sharp bits of steel, topped by frothing tails of ice that came and went. Martin shivered and pulled the dark-blue sailcloth curtains closed, knotting them shut with the string ties Teresa had sewn on when it became obvious that they could not stuff enough newspaper in the rotting window frames to keep the night from howling through. As much as he might like to watch the rush of storm – there was something exhilarating about the muscularity of the waves – he needed to keep the room warm for Teresa and the baby, if the baby's first taste of air were to be anything but ice. Early this morning, way before the wind had collected its rat minions to spar with the desperate waves, he had heard Teresa utter a soft sharp cry. Then, she had put her knee against his back and nudged him ever so gently.

"Today," she said, squeezing his arm before guiding his hand backwards to her extended belly. When he felt that her muscles had gathered into a hard raised spine, he had rolled over so that he might see her eyes. She had looked him with a stillness both reassuring and somewhat disconcerting.

"You okay?" Her eyes were almost tunnels -- dark, deep and without any exit. He wanted desperately to see again her eyes marked with a familiar lucid spark, but it was as if Teresa had been pulled inward to some echoing undersea cavern he could not reach. When finally she resurfaced, she smiled, contraction passed, and he relaxed. He was glad the smile was not fleeting. As she drew her lips upward into a smile, she exhaled, blowing a steady stream of warm breath that settled into a pool in the hollow between his shoulder and his neck. Her smile stayed and grew until it had absorbed both cheeks, her nose, her ears, and all of him. He felt as if he were swimming again in the warm waters of the Pacific where they had lived for so many years before coming to this grey rocky coast. He closed his eyes and saw a turtle swim a slow parentheses atop the reef.

"I'm fine. Really. Just working hard, staying with it." Teresa laid her palm gently on his upper arm and closed her eyes. "It's hard, you know, when a body decides to do something without the mind. We humans forget we live in bodies, especially those of us more comfortable using our minds."

Teresa's fingers danced past his ear and down his neck. He arched up to meet her mouth. She was the most beautiful woman he had ever seen, his mermaid, his dream. They had met on an isolated atoll in the south Pacific where he was mapping the geologic records of ancient tsunamis and Teresa was living quietly in a tin-roofed shack near the shoreline, rising every day with the sun to write and tend her overgrown garden of sweet potatoes, beans and squash planted inside a semicircle of papaya trees, some bearing, others still reaching for the sky. Beyond the little garden was another tin-roofed shack, but this one, unlike hers, had no screens. A bandy-legged nanny goat lived in one side and in the other half a dozen plus chickens roosted each night on a wide ladder made of peeled hau branches twined together with nylon rope. Judging from the color and size of the various bits of rope, Martin assumed that the rope had been salvaged from the flotsam and jetsam that washed ashore, and later Teresa had confirmed this for him.

She had taken him to the tiny cove where the currents brought ashore the best of the sea treasures, showed him the shallow cave where she sorted and stored what the ocean brought – piles of plastic bottles, some still useful as containers, some suitable only for cutting into scoops or sun shields for baby plants; planks of wood for building and battered tree limbs that might be used as fence posts; bits of metal and glass, and several entire glass bottles so worn by the tumble of the tides that they resembled ancient Etruscan wine bottles. She called it her octopus's garden in the shade.

Martin had come to the island to record the world as it existed, but Teresa had come to record what she dreamed and what she remembered, true or not. Everyday, she wrote stories in blue-lined notebooks that she kept in an old biscuit tin stored on a shelf above her bed. Later, after she had brewed many cups of tea and he had cooked several dinners of broiled fish and seaweed, Teresa told him that she had first come to the island as a Peace Corps volunteer ten years previous, before the tsunami, when the shoreline had been crowded with fishing villages, the tangled hau trees shrouded with drying nets, and the cove alive with any number of brightly painted boats. After a bitter and painful divorce, she had returned, hoping to write what she remembered of those days but had found herself writing imagined tales instead. At first, she had been unwilling to read him her stories, but one night when the skies were crystal clear and the Milky Way as broad and wide as he had ever seen it, even in the thin mountain air of the Rocky Mountains, they sat under swaying oil lamps suspended from the rafters of her house while she read a tiny story about an eel that had come ashore and surprised a young fisherman who had been cleaning fish on a rock jutting into the waves. It was a simple story but beautifully told.

As she read, he could smell the water, feel the heat of the sun as it glanced from the rocking waves to the sleek blue black slither of the eel as it edged its way over the lava, hoping for some part of the newly cleaned fish. When the young boy flicked fish intestine towards the eel with its gaping mouth, Martin had laughed, not just because the gesture was so kind but because he realized at that moment that he loved Teresa uncontrollably and completely.

"Martin?" Teresa was looking at him, her chin resting on her hand. "Martin, where are you? You're drifting again, my sweet. I need you here, need you to call the midwives, please. Our baby wants to meet you."

"And you." Martin ran his hand through Teresa's hair.

"Oh, Martin, she already knows me, inside and out." Teresa laughed. "Okay, maybe she knows me pretty well *inside*, needs to meet the out."

"She?"

Teresa just smiled, but then her mouth circled tight and her eyes creased shut. Another contraction.

Martin leaped up, pulled on his jeans, and turned to Teresa.

"Breathe, honey. The midwives will soon be here. Promise."

Months ago when they were still in the Pacific, dreaming of staying alone and happy on that little atoll, Teresa had told him she wanted to birth her baby at home, and he had been startled. Not because she wanted to have a home birth – he had been born at home in the middle of a fierce thunderstorm – but that she wanted to have a baby. He had felt suddenly and quite unexpectedly dizzingly happy, overwhelmed by a sparking light that whistled through his body in waves, leaving every cell it touched at the edge of transformation. Blood melted to air; bone threatened to bloom, and he was enclosed by a gold net of the finest weave. Later, he decided what he had passed through and what had passed through him was joy.

Teresa was already pregnant when he was offered the job at Woods Hole, and they decided it was time to return to the States. When they arrived, they had asked about a midwife, but initially received either questions or stern admonishments in response to their queries. They had just about given up when a young mother Teresa had met while walking down by the harbor told her about Yasmin and her sister Iris who had recently moved to town from Boston where they had been delivering babies, mostly in Roxbury and Somerville, for the past twenty-five years. They were, she said, alert, professional, kind, and they always arrived with everything needed in case of an emergency. Together, the young mother had told Teresa, Yasmin and Iris had successfully delivered more than three hundred babies, and every year in September, they always staged a picnic "reunion" of mothers, fathers, and babies on Cape Cod. It was always quite the scene – babies, toddlers, teenagers, and now young adults with their own babies. Second generation home deliveries. They were their own tribe. Would Teresa and Martin like to go to the picnic as her guest?

It had all seemed too perfect, but Martin and Teresa had grown used to sudden and seemingly inexplicable events that offered solution or at least resolution rather than problem. After the picnic, after spending time with Yasmin and Iris and their dozens and dozens of "children," Teresa met with the midwives twice a month, learning as much as she could about the process of birth – what to expect and what she could do to help her body bring her baby into the world. She learned that primarily she would have to trust the wisdom of her body and act in support of that wisdom and strength, if she wanted her baby to emerge joyfully rather than painfully.

They had spoken of underwater births, all the rage, it seemed, but had decided that despite their love of waves and water, they weren't fish and that as their baby would breathe air, she should be born into air. Some transitions, Martin had said, are better made speedily. Teresa had agreed. Of course, she later told Yasmin, if she happened to be snorkeling when the baby decided to arrive, she would be born in water, but the chances that she would be snorkeling in the Atlantic in January were close to zero. In fact, she doubted that she would ever snorkel in that grey chop. She wondered what she would see if she snorkeled through the cove at the height of summer. Codfish? Ancient wrecks? Rusting barrels of who knows what tipped into disintegrating tires?

Unlike the turquoise Pacific, the waters of the Atlantic seemed to hide more than they revealed, and today was no exception. Martin peeked through the slit of the closed curtains, noting that the chop on the sea was even more confused than it been earlier. If the waves had looked like swarms of rats before, now they looked like possums clambering wildly over one another. He glanced left and then right, looking from one end of the street to the other, wanting to see the flash of Yasmin's familiar pink sedan with its trunk and back fenders painted white to resemble a neatly pinned diaper, a pink pin on the top side of one fender, a blue on the other. With all this sleet and ice, he hoped the midwives would not have difficulty navigating the hill at the far edge of town, often difficult in weather such as this. He paced nervously, opening and closing the curtain so many times, that he finally left it open to the push of sea and sky. On a day like this, the pace of storm could not be excluded.

By the time Yasmin and Iris arrived, the contractions had inexplicably slowed, but the teakettle was boiling and the room warm. Martin was glad he had opened the curtains; the patterning of light as it sifted through clouds seemed in harmony with the Bach breathing through the radio. Iris explained that the slowing of contractions was to be expected, especially for a first birth, that Teresa's body was resting. Then, as Yasmin bustled about setting up the emergency equipment, Martin set the table with Teresa's grandmother's hand-painted bone china.

Although he was too flustered (excited might be a better word) to cook eggs, he had baked two loaves of walnut-apricot bread yesterday, and that, together with the tea, would provide a morning meal for everyone while they waited for the contractions to start up again, which they did by late morning. This second tidal wave of contractions was much faster, far more ferocious. Each contraction coming more frequently than anyone could have predicted. As that tide swelled, the rosy rhythms of the morning disappeared behind rising storm and the raucous waves that continued to surge and crash beyond the window. No longer possums, Martin thought. They're donkeys now, kicking out the jams.

The intensity of these new contractions surprised Teresa, and the desperation in her sudden cries surprised Martin. At first, he collapsed against the sharpness of her cries. He felt paralyzed, useless. He just couldn't stand to hear her pain crying out, but after Iris shot him several potent looks, he recovered. He remembered the stages of birth, recalled what Yasmin had told Teresa, that labor was called labor for a reason. It was *hard work,* and hard work is rarely comfortable, if she could remember when the contractions came hard and fast, as they were now, that her body was *working, laboring,* as hard as it could to save her and the baby from any unnecessary pain, she might help her body do the work it needed to do.

Martin needed to help Teresa help her body. All her blood was rushing from her brain to her abdomen; he needed to lend her his brain, his reason. He pulled himself gently away from his own fears, listening instead to the calm steady voices of Yasmin and Iris who were repeating in harmony, *breathe breathe breathe,* and breathe he did.

He began to breathe as Yasmin had taught them both to breathe, inhaling slowly and deeply as the contraction began, exhaling as the muscles began to lose their tension. With his hand resting lightly on Teresa's stomach, he could feel her muscles tense and then relax. If he breathed in concert with those contractions, he might help Teresa know when to inhale and when to exhale. As he changed his own rhythms, Teresa too abandoned her sharp staccato gasping to join the warm curve of his deep steady breathing. When finally they were breathing with as much strength as the wind now pushing waves ashore, as much power as the repeated humming of *breathe breathe breathe,* Martin gathered Teresa's hand gently in his and quietly massaged her fingers, one by one, moving easily from inhale to exhale. He linked his energy to hers and watched as anxiety in her eyes turned to concentration and then to something he later described to her as bliss.

"Yes," she later said, "that was bliss. Giving birth was bliss. The joy arrived only when I held our baby in my arms. Then, oh . . ."

Somehow Martin was not surprised that when the moment of the birth arrived, the radio was playing Vivaldi's Concerto in C, "In Trompa Marina." It seemed entirely natural that their daughter would take her first breath accompanied by a lute playing music written for the "sea trumpet." If he had had a conch, he would have breathed and breathed until his lungs were bursting, then wrapped his lips around the narrow neck of the shell and let all his breath escape as a long low note rising to the thin tenor held by the wind. Then, he would have let his voice rest on that wind.

"The tides have shifted," he would have cried, "the storm has settled, and Marina is born!"

Space Between

I'm not sure I can tell you how I felt when I woke up on the street, my head resting on a black plastic garbage bag, but I'm going to try. Before I opened my eyes, I could feel the sun burrowing into my skin, not sharply like a knife but softly like rum on a buttercake. That made me hungry, I guess, so I scratched about looking for the cookies I usually leave on my bedside table every night just in case I wake needing late night nibbles, but my fingers never found the polished wood of that table. Instead, they raked across a rough stubble of concrete and closed on something that felt suspiciously like bits of broken glass. If I tell you that it was only then that I opened my eyes, you'll realize that I must have spent the night quite unconscious and alone.

When I opened my eyes, all I could see was blue – a turquoise sky washed above me, thin blue curls of what seemed at first to be smoke rising from car bumpers, blue-painted fence posts, battered blue plastic garbage cans, a blue glaze like spider webs settled over the brick walls and the window panes of the building across the street. I suppose it was that blue smoke that made me think at first (irrationally, I know) that I was in Hell, but it is a testament to my sanity and my will to live, I guess, that I quickly realized that it was not smoke but water vapor, last night's heavy dew evaporating upwards with the heat of the morning sun.

When I tried to roll over and push myself from the pavement, a sharp pain wired up my back and lodged itself somewhere beneath my left ear. The pain was so intense, I could not locate it. I didn't know if it was the moving of my arm or the shifting of my hips that caused that lightning bolt, so I began slowly to investigate. I wiggled my toes inside my socks and realized rather quickly I had no shoes. I moved my fingers, one by one, and when I tried lifting my arms, one by one, I found I could. Independently, each floated easily upwards. If I had been surrounded by water, I would have been swimming, but when I tried again to turn and push myself from the ground, the pain knifed through. I think I cried out because at that moment I heard a woman's voice, clanging like some ill-tuned bell. *Come away, dear. The man's drunk.*

Her shoes sounded crisp and clean on the concrete, heels providing intentional accents to her words. I could tell she was trying to speed by, but I didn't know whom she addressed. I wanted to know so I kept my face turned in the general direction of her voice, saw first silk-clad legs and the folded cuffs of red leather ankle boots, then smaller bare legs with tinier feet stuffed into grubby sneakers, and finally, after they had walked some paces across the street, I could see a face looking back. A small face with wide blue eyes balanced above pink cheeks disappearing under a field of white blond curls. I would have sworn that that little face had a halo of light hovering about her, but I suppose I wouldn't have sworn that in court. I imagine it was just the early morning sun sparking off newly washed hair and something about the crystalline quality of the air.

Everything did seem brighter somehow, edges more distinct, colors crisper. Sounds were as transparent, as fragile as glass. I swear I could hear the woman breathing – not just the ragged sighs leaving her body but the soft swilling of air in her lungs. I could hear the alveoli hissing and the pleural fluid sloshing about like sea waves lapping the sands of a placid lagoon. The girl's heart sounded like a tiny bird singing.

I tried to call out, but my tongue seemed melted in my mouth and when I tried to move the overgrown sea slug it had become, it slipped against my lip and not my teeth. My teeth, like my shoes, were gone. I do know that I wondered then if they had been stolen or smashed. Considering the size of my tongue, I voted for the latter rather than the former. By then, after all, I was awake and thinking rationally. I remember thinking, quite calmly, that smashed dentures were no problem. I had a spare set at home, stored in a black lacquer box in the back of my sock drawer. Of course, there was a problem. Without teeth and with a swollen tongue, I couldn't speak. If I tried, words emerged as grunts and moans, completely formless, quite meaningless, so I suppose I shouldn't blame the woman with red boots for tugging at her small daughter's hand and moving quickly by. She made an active (and probably rational) decision to protect her daughter and speed on by, figuring, no doubt, that soon I would wake and go about my gin-soaked life, that there was nothing she could do about it.

At least she noticed me, which is more than I can say for most of the sleepwalkers who passed without breaking stride, without saying a word, without even looking down. I wanted them to see me. I wanted them to help me, but they moved dazedly down the street, stopping at the street corner only when passing traffic wouldn't let them cross.

After trying once or twice to wake them – I even tossed a pebble at the shoe of one (as best I could), gestured at another – I gave up. I know a bit about sleepwalking, especially how dangerous and disorienting it can be to wake up suddenly in the middle of a nighttime prowl, or in this case, an early morning stroll. I once had a psychology professor deliver a whole lecture on that topic, going on and on about some female patient of his who had appeared in his office so confused and dazed he'd thought he would have to hospitalize her but when she lapsed suddenly into the rapid disconnected speech so common with sleepwalkers, he had theorized that she'd been abruptly awakened while sleepwalking and was now frozen in some state between wakefulness and sleep, unable to function in one or another. He'd solved her "mental" dilemma with hypnosis, allowing her to return mentally to the locale of midnight stroll and then moving her gently ever so gently to wakefulness. When she awoke, she was once again fully present and functioning in the world of sun and shade.

After class, my friend Mark scoffed and sneered at this professor who had his doctorate from a university where they only taught behaviorism. *What a crock,* he said. *Why do I have to listen to this drivel?* Mark dropped the class, but I stayed in. I knew what the professor had said was more than interesting. It might even have been profound, but then I was always more the theorist, the one interested in how things worked. Mark didn't like puzzling through things. He wanted to know systems, beginning, ends, middles, what connected to what, learn the discoveries of others so that he might fix easily that which could be fixed and forget about the rest. He's the one who became the surgeon; I stayed with the unknowable.

Even then in graduate school, I had had some experience with sleepwalkers, and perhaps my experience made me listen just a little more intently to what the professor was saying than did Mark. Mark dismissed his story as exaggeration; I accepted it as truth. Been there, done that. After all, my younger brother had been a sleepwalker, and I had once watched my mother wake my brother using a method similar to the one our professor described in class. No hypnosis but the same gradual introduction of the real into the imagined. I remember that night as clearly as I now recall my morning lying on the sun-soaked sidewalk while the zombie sleepwalkers walked on past, even stepping over me if need be.

The night of my brother's sleepwalking excursion we'd been visiting my grandmother, a retired nurse who still lived in the modest house my grandfather had built on the beach when he was working during the week as a longshoreman in town and surfing the break out front on weekends. Their house, like so many built at the edge of the sea before the days of gated communities and locked gates, backed on a busy street, rumbling with trucks. If you didn't mind the kids gunning the motors of their low riders, the road was great for an easy commute to town. Not so great, however, for sleepwalkers. Too many impromptu road races.

Brian, my brother, was a sweet kid, almost ten years younger than me, a rambunctious sort who loved water and waves. I stayed in and read, but Brian had learned to swim at the age of three, and two years later just shy of his fifth birthday, he was learning to surf. The morning of his famous night travels, he had actually managed to stand on the board and make it all the way to shore without falling. Our grandpa first taught Brian how to balance by laying the board on the sand, playing music and asking Brian to balance on the back of the chords. Brian learned to surf music before he even tried waves. He was determined.

He loved the sea and all creatures who lived in it. His favorite song was the Beatles' "Octopus' Garden." *I want to be under the sea in an octopus' garden in the shade.* His attachment to that song was exactly what worried my Mom when he came into the kitchen that night first humming and speaking rapidly words pushed together in a way that might have seemed nonsensical except that my mother knew that Beatles' tune as well as did Brian. There was logic to his speech, but his mind was moving too fast for his tongue. Whole phrases dropped out. *I want to be under the sea in an octopus' garden in the shade* became, quite sensibly, *I be octopus shade.*

Brian's feet were moving as fast as was his brain. His legs couldn't keep up with his feet, his hips lagged behind his legs. He danced impossibly across the floor, and like some tree frog thrown down on desert sand, he headed straight for the door, his tiny body twisting this way and that, hands outstretched as if he were already on the waves. The minute he was out the door, my mother followed, one finger to her lips, the fingers of her other hand waving me to follow as well. She didn't want Brian ending up in any octopus' garden in the shade, tucked deep under ocean waves.

She stayed between Brian and the shore break, and gestured to me that I should keep track of his other side, making sure he didn't surf his way up onto a neighbor's potted palm or venture between houses to the busy street behind. Halfway down the beach, my mother waved her hand, asking me to run interference, slow his pace as she moved closer to Brian, shifting his path further from tide line and closer to the houses. Suddenly, she was in front of him, causing him to turn more sharply towards me. She was herding him home.

I watched Brian pass in front of me with my mother still between him and the waves. She was one current; I was another, and together we directed him home. Back in the kitchen, while I darted this way, like some big fish, keeping Brian from again heading out the door, my mother grabbed a glass from the sink, went to the fridge and pulled out a carton of milk. Then, when Brian surfed her way, still muttering about the octopus' garden, she held out a glass half-full of milk. Amazingly, he took it and drank it. As he drank, I watched the blue glaze fall from his eyes with every swallow. It was as if a curtain were being drawn open. The shade disappeared. I would swear his skin moved from white to pink, his eyes blinked twice, and then he was awake. He stared down at the empty glass in his hand and then looked first at our mother and then at me. Clearly he was puzzled, but just as I was about to explain, our mother put her finger again to her lips. She knelt beside Brian and gathered him in her arms. He nestled into her neck, and she lifted him and carried him back to bed, tucked him and in and then kissed him goodnight. He was soon as sound asleep dreaming oceans as he had been wide-awake sleepwalking songs.

Lying there, that morning on the sidewalk with my huge tongue trying to find a way out of my mouth, I thought about that night. I wondered (quite illogically, of course) if I too had been out surfing some terrestrial wave, but without the loving protective currents my mother and I had offered Brian. Had I surfed at speed into some blind rock canyon, also home to stampeding stallions? All this puzzling kept me lucid as the morning commuters bustled by, but by noon, the shooting pain at first felt only when I tried to move had become a creeping ache that would not go away. I knew something was very very wrong. I needed help.

What had been blue sky at dawn was now littered with shooting stars, red, green gold, every color of the rainbow except grey. I needed to awaken at least one of the sleepwalking zombies if I were to return to the church and my parishioners. I abandoned my reverie of surf breaks and tried to remember how to form words in a mouth without teeth, but then as quickly as that pain had lodged itself behind my ear, I realized I didn't need words. I lifted my arm but instead of gesturing uselessly to the passers-by, I reached up and slowly unbuttoned the top button of my overcoat. I felt inside to see if by any chance I had been wearing my clerical collar whenever whatever had happened to me. If I had been lying with my head on this black plastic bag for one evening and one night only, chances were I had my collar on. The last thing I remembered was welcoming parishioners to our annual Christmas pageant at the church, and I always made sure I was pressed and collared for that extravaganza.

This year had been rather low key actually. All the little ones had dressed as elves; the teenage boys were reindeer and the older girls dressed in ankle length white gowns lit up the room as breathtaking angels with silver tinfoil wings, too tiny to support flight but just right to catch the light. One member of my church, Dan, worked on off-Broadway shows and he had rigged up some spots with colored gels in the rec room. Marissa, a reindeer mother, had decorated the whole room with tinsel garlands and some sprigs of mistletoe with papier-maché berries and construction-paper leaves, three colors of green. Very pretty. A long table set up against the wall was for coats, another on the opposite wall had two huge bowls of punch and plates and plates of home-made cookies. As there was no crèche, no magi, no Mary, the angels, elves, and reindeer had decided together to sing about Frosty and Rudolf but were adamant that "Silent Night" would signal the end of the pageant and the beginning of the feast.

I touched my neck and felt first the soft wool of my scarf but underneath my thumb brushed the starched stiffness of the collar. I'll tell you at that moment, I could hear a low humming in my ears that I'll swear to you was the future speaking of the past. So smooth that voice, kind and forgiving. Slowly ever so slowly I loosened my scarf, eased it back from my neck, straightened my collar as best I could, and shifted my body ever so slightly and ever so painfully so my coat stayed open and the collar stayed visible.

Lunch hour was ending. Soon the legs would begin swaying on by again, but I was hopeful that now someone would stop. After all, my collar was screaming loud and clear. Sure enough, the very first person who got within four feet of me stopped and peered down at me with great concern penciled on her brow. I can describe that face – a smooth oval with pale grey eyes flecked with lavender, a tiny mole at the corner of her mouth. So beautiful, I tried to say something. I couldn't help myself even knowing that my jumbled speech might frighten her as much as it had the young woman with the red boots. Of course, my attempts at speech produced nothing but mumbles sounding like gas explosions, but my grinding grunts didn't alarm her. Instead, she laid her hand gently on my forehead and turned to the second face peering down from above.

"Run," she said to the young man standing next to her.

"Run get help."

And run he did.

Soon there were more concerned faces, more
gentle voices, a cup of water at my lips, and a siren still far but approaching, closer closer by the minute. I squeezed the hand of whomever it was whose hand had been laid on mine and tried to smile. I don't think I succeeded but if I had, there would have to have been something exceedingly sad about that smile, if not sad then tragic or worse, fake maybe even diabolical. Yes, I was finally safe. I would live. But only because I had been long enough on the sidewalk to strategize. Only because I thought to expose my collar. Help came when my "position," if you want to call it that, had been exposed.

I tell you this story with great difficulty because I know clearly and painfully that without that marker of place, without that symbol of my position in the community, voices had been rough. I had even felt a few surreptitious kicks throughout the morning hours, usually followed by a snicker and once an arch *pardon me your highness, pardonnez moi*. I can't even count how many were willing to just let me lie there, maybe even die there, but with the collar exposed, I was deemed worthy of life. Exposing my heart, my need had not been enough. I needed a badge, a name-tag to survive.

Slow River

There are days when I wake only partially. My eyes open but I feel as if I am looking at the world through a series of curtains, each imprinted with a silk-screened snapshot of some corner of another world. Nothing spectacular – a newspaper stand, an ATM machine, red-cheeked kids fishing, men in long dark overcoats walking down a rutted road, a rotting pier in some city I don't recognize, a bronze wolf cemented to a narrow walk near a decrepit logcabin made picturesque with newly planted riotous 'wild' flowers in pots. Okay, maybe that last image is a bit out there. After all, how many bronze wolves are there in port cities?

The only one I know is the one that skulks about ten feet or so from the Jack London's 'reconstructed' wilderness cabin in downtown Oakland. Reconstructed, my ass. If those logs were trucked down from Alaska, I was cracked out of an egg. I swear on all that I hold dear, including my 1966 World Series baseball, that cabin is one built for Charlie Chaplin's *Goldrush*, rejected for various obvious insufficiencies and then stored for years on a prop lot on the outskirts of Sacramento before some stoner had one of those smoky flashes of brilliance, deciding to dust it off and give it a new life as Jack London's writing hideaway. No way London wrote anything in that drafty lean-to. He would have been far too busy keeping warm.

Anyway, I'm veering off track here. The only reason I mentioned that bronze wolf sneaking about outside that bogus cabin is that when I close my eyes, I see it rearing up like a hungry dragon (the wolf, that is, not the cabin), leaving me no recourse except to spit it out here on paper, get rid of it anyway I can. What good are bronze wolves out back of an old shack that shivers and shakes when temperatures fall to 60 degrees Fahrenheit?

I have no idea why that image is first and foremost now except that maybe flying three thousand miles and arriving close to midnight was a bad idea. Transitions are difficult when driving in the dark. No way to make sense of difference because difference is masked by dark. It was dark; I arrived. End of story.

But not. The story's just beginning.

I sleep, wake, and nothing makes real sense.

I know I am elsewhere, but the elsewhere is both achingly familiar and extraordinarily strange and unreachable. It's as if the 'real' just up and left somewhere midstream, just like that goddam wolf or maybe it *is* the cabin, after all, rearing up and slipping off the cliff. All I can grasp are glimmering images, skeletal bits of light and dark, not always readable on the silken sleeves they're printed on, a bit like what sailors see when staring at waves too still too flat too hot for way too many days. Mermaids with graceful arms, undersea kings with scepters that poke at blinking stars, elusive images that come and go, imposing themselves on the horizon line, masquerading as rescue boats. Here, the sirens are racing headlong down the street on the velvet black of my gratefully still closed eyes. And these sirens are real, all too real.

Shadows, I guess. Like me, I guess.

How many once described *me* like that? Nothing but a shadow. An ex-monk wandering about the countryside for years, looking for a flock. Well, I guess that shadow has grown wings, dense or luminous, your call. I have that flock now, but I'm not the shepherd and they don't worship me or Jesus or anybody. They learn to love themselves, and that's enough. Funny thing about love. If you love yourself, it's easier not harder to love others. Loving one's self is a helluva lot different from worshipping one's self.

Day and night, light and dark, so it seems.

I left the church only shortly after joining it, several lifetimes ago. I joined because I needed love in my life and left for the same reason. I fell in love or lust (who knows about those things) with a young nun who had the most tender tawny skin and a sweet face lit by jeweled eyes that sparked even in the dark. I suppose under different circumstances, I might have approached the bump-a-thump-bump in my groin as one of those tests of the flesh except that she fell in love with me, too.

There was no stopping us. We gazed into each other's eyes during mass, snuck into the chapel after hours and made love at the feet of the Virgin Mary with the baby Jesus looking on. Next thing we knew Maria, that *was* her name, was facing the daunting task of explaining yet another virgin birth to her Mother Superior. As that prospect seemed a bit over the top, we gave it up, left our 'habits', so to speak, folded neatly at the door and went hand-in-hand towards the sunset, feeling every inch like the Tramp and the Gamin in Chaplin's *Modern Times*. We were on our way.

As it turned out, that way was pretty much a blind alley, used for the disposal of all kinds of trash and home to any number of sharp-fanged rats. We went giggling in and came out staggering. The baby didn't make it and neither did we. Maria ended up back at the convent, weeping, and I ended up counting cards in Las Vegas, made some money, lost more, always asking God to make up the difference, which, of course, never happened. When prayer failed to change the odds, I went to work, burning the midnight oil, learning how to dress for success, how to turn my face to steel, how to *really* count cards. Soon, I was good, very good, making thousands every night, donating to charity half of what I raked in, just in case God had something to do with it after all. Seemed idyllic, but then, what can I say? I got cocky and the casinos got tough. The boss men dressed to the nines in their hand-made Italian suits with button-down cuffs don't like folks beating them at their own game, and they sure as hell don't like some Irish punk waltzing in the door wearing the exact same suit down to the lapel pin as the head honcho. That probably wasn't too smart. In fact, that may have been my biggest mistake.

I could have gone on winning against the house for just a bit longer, I think, had I pretended I was some poor gas station attendant, wearing acid-washed jeans and grease-stained Hotel California T-shirts, but, of course, I was too full of myself for that. I was one helluva stuffed shirt. I can tell you that.

I had God on my side, after all. Maybe, anyway. After my big night at the MGM Grand – I was winning big and making quite a show of it, buying the best champagne for everyone within earshot – the wizard behind the screen put out his own version of an APB, complete with photos, and suddenly, there was no more room at the inn for me.

I must admit – I didn't take their warnings too seriously at first. I kept trying to weasel in, mix with the Kansas yokels. I even dressed like a church lady one night, white gloves, high-heels, a full skirt and even fuller blue-tinted hair but I didn't make it past the slot machines. The bouncer who bounced about with the four-armed bandits grabbed my elbow and said, "Sam," that's what I called myself those days, "You make one helluva ugly broad." After delivering that one-liner, he winked, gave me a big smooch on my cheek, and showed me the door. Messed up my make-up.

I went home, popped a beer, kicked off my tasteful heels, and sat on the couch until dawn, thinking about the over-sized holster Mr. No-Name bouncer had flashed before pushing me out the door. I kept wondering exactly what fit into that thing. And so I arrived at the end of my card-counting career.

I suppose it might have been the end of me had I not figured out *why* I was such a good counter. That night I tried making mental lists of my skills, but in the end, I could only find one skill worth listing. I was a good listener, and nothing is more important to successful politicking than listening. And no one makes more money in this country than politicians. If I wanted to get my hands on some money, make a difference in this world, I would just have to step onto the political stage. And so I did. Actually I danced my way onto that stage. At first I was more of a jester than a magician but after a while I was holed up in the smoky back rooms, listening.

Believe it or not, I had learned the art of silent listening in the monastery. I swear I could hear rats singing to one another through brick walls, the whispers of clouds passing overhead. No surprise, then, that I could hear the cards. Listening is good. More than a skill, it is an addition. A good listener remembers, and a good counter remembers distinctly. I add that last because I want you to know, dear reader, that what I am telling you is the truth, so help me Dog, nothing but the truth. It wasn't school and it certainly wasn't monastic life that made it possible for me to be doing what I am doing today. It was listening.

First, I listened to the cards in a deck and then I listened to the 'cards' who loitered *on* the deck, all those puffed-up self-absorbed power brokers who run the ship of state. What I'd heard would curl your hair, but I'm not going to repeat any of that. I've been called a lot of things in my life but 007 isn't one of them. What I will tell you, what I can tell you, is that most of those men strutting about on the poop deck with thumbs tucked in their belt were not nice folk. Just as you can always tell something about a man by watching how he treats women and children, you can always tell something about an institution by examining how those in the upper echelons treat those who scurry about on the lower decks, how they use the power granted them.

What I saw made me sick to my stomach and, I must admit, after spending time with those folks, after hears their all their Machiavellian bullshit, I just wanted to pick up and leave again, live well away from the madding crowd, but I didn't go to the mountaintop, if that's what you're thinking. Sitting in some cave meditating on my navel would be an action just as self-absorbed as the hand shakes of those who strutted about the hallways of the legislature, passing laws that suited them and forgetting about real people who struggled to live on annual incomes one-tenth or less of what those fat cats raked in every month.

I didn't go back to the monastery either. Instead, I got lost in the ghetto, went to work as a day laborer and then a carpenter, rented a tiny flat in a section of town where few, other than the most easily forgotten, venture. Across the street was Leo's Auto Repair, a lot empty except for a windowless shack and two rusting and wheel-less pick-up trucks. Leo came and went, arriving daily around noon to unbolt the gate, which was never left open for customers. Predictably, there were no customers. No car customers anyway. No smoking sedans. No broken down trucks. 'Leo,' if that was his name, which I doubt, always parked his late-model BMW sports car inside the 8' high fence topped with razor-wire, well away from the shed and under a green tarp. Even though the fence had been covered with corrugated tin, I knew this because I lived on the fourth floor and could easily stare into that 'auto repair' lot. I could see the sewer rats run the fence, and I could see other more nattily dressed rats come and go by special signal every Thursday promptly at 10 a.m.

Thursdays, the dynamic duo – two police detectives dressed in their spiffiest street clothes, jackets gapped just enough to allow a sneak peak of their gun holsters – rattled the fence, and every Thursday, Leo would let them in, after standing for several minutes in the open doorway, blocking their way and their view of the open lot behind him. Leo had them trained like the dogs that they were. He always waited until one of the two fidgeted and glanced backward over his shoulder. Then, he raised his hand and with a suspiciously mocking sweeping gesture, waved them in. Of course, at first time they arrived, I wondered what was going on, but frankly, I didn't have to wonder long.

The detectives left by noon, and five minutes later, the 'real' customers arrived – mostly wispy girls with bone thin arms and mismatched shoes, some nervous young men, and late model cars with out-of-state plates. Crack addicts and low-level dealers. Leo and his law-enforcement buddies were working hard to keep things settled and sedated in the ghetto and getting rich in process.

The day I saw one of those bone tired teenagers sidle through gate with an equally thin and obviously hungry toddler riding on her sharp-boned hip was the day that tore it for me. I was ready to grab my baseball bat and rush over there, give Leo a bit of another kind of medicine that might leave him as incapacitated as these kids he was supplying with drugs, drugs and more drugs. I caught hold of myself before doing anything foolish. Baseball bats can't really win in a game of rock-paper-scissors where guns are involved, but I did promise myself, then and there, that I would get to Leo, stop the dealing. I knew I had to strategize.

As it turned out, I didn't need to figure anything out after all. All I had to do was be in the right place at the right time and act. Simple as that. I had a carpentry job a few blocks away. We were reinforcing the roof beams on a warehouse, marrying 2 x12s to the existing rafters and building cross bracing. The guy who bought the warehouse had some cockamamie idea that he was going to build a tower on the roof so that he might watch the stars at night and the harbor during the day, but the roof had to be strengthened first. Those of us willing and able to inch our way out on narrow beams 15 feet above concrete floors have a decided advantage over those who tremble at the edge of things. I was getting paid well and enjoyed a certain amount of freedom on the jobsite. I had even built myself a little aerie up amongst the roof beams where I would sit and mediate every morning before dragging out the scaffolding and getting down to the business of heavy lifting. It was a sweet little cubbyhole with a cushion for my skinny behind and comfortable leather backrest borrowed from some old junk pickup abandoned down by the docks.

Well, to make a long story short, I was sitting up there early one morning, well before 9 a.m., when I heard someone turning the key in the lock of the front door. I thought it was a just bit early for Angela — she ordinarily appeared mid-morning after feeding her kids and getting them off to school. I peered over the edge of my nest and was surprised to see one member of the dynamic duo minus his camel hair coat but with a neatly wrapped bundle tucked under his arm.

I kept still, hardly even daring to take a breath, and watched as he shoved the old battered couch aside and pried up a section of the floor. The ease with which he lifted that piece of floor made me realize that this was something he'd done before. If you are assuming that he placed his wrapped package there, replaced the floor, and left, you'd be right. That is exactly what happened, but what happened later surprised me and changed my life and the lives of more people than I care to count.

Angela arrived as usual about 10 a.m. but just as she set her things down in the office and switched the computer on, the *second* member of the dynamic duo burst through the door, gun drawn. He grabbed Angela and started ranting and raving about some mugger he'd seen slip into the warehouse. He put his gun to her head and threatened to blow her brains out if she didn't tell him where to find this 'miserable cur,' as he called him, but Angela's one cool cookie, street wise and tough. I suspect that wasn't the first time she had a gun pointed at her temple. She didn't flinch – just looked Mr. Detective straight in the eyes, pointed to her coat, her purse and her diamond ring, stated (quite logically actually) that if there were a mugger about, she hadn't seen him. Then, she invited the cop, who by now had flashed his badge, to look about. He would, she said, find few places to hide in the open space beyond. He looked, of course, in the one closet, under the desk, between the stacks of wood, but he never looked up. He found nothing and nobody. Then, he grumbled his apologies to Angela who by then was fixing coffee. She offered him a cup, but he just snarled and left.

After I was quite sure he was gone, I climbed down from my aerie and told Angela what I had seen. I also told her what I knew about the dynamic duo and their nefarious dealings across the street from my apartment and just what I suspicioned might be in that package secreted in its neat little hidey-hole beneath the floorboards. I was hoping cash, fearing drugs.

We waited, Angela and I, until all was quiet on the western front and then we slid the couch back, opened the floor, measured the package carefully so that we might make one at least somewhat close to original. We'd switch the packages, open the original, decide what to do. It was risky but, all in all, a good plan.

We were patient. We were quiet. We changed the locks so that cop #1 couldn't let himself in with his key. Didn't really matter -- we didn't figure he was coming back real soon – but we needed to keep the ruse from being exposed too soon. We did know his 'partner' would be tracking him closely for a while. We did know he would have to lay low, feign innocence. The way we had it figured by the time he managed to weasel his way back in to his hidey-hole, retrieved the package and and discovered the switch, the job in the rafters would be finished and we would have figured out the next step.

Lucky for us what was in the package was cash, not drugs. Drugs we would have heaved, but we saw no reason to return so much cash to known drug dealers, especially those who worked on the side of the law. I wish I could say that when I told Angela what I intended to do with my share, she wanted in and that we flew down here like one big happy family, but that's too Hollywood. Angela wanted her share for her kids – who can blame her – and I wanted my share for mine.

We both knew that my kids were far more numerous, that they would move on only when ready, so we split 2/3 -1/3, and off I went. Seek and ye shall find, so goes the saying, and I did find a beautiful rambling house on a placid river not too far from the coast. Green green waters and green green trees. Live oaks dripping with Spanish moss, citrus trees overwhelmed by ripening fruit. Piney woods nearby to clean the air. The flowers I planted that first year now spill down riverbanks and fill once empty fields in summer, and together the kids and I carved paths into the hammock lands, built shelters where we can watch the forest come and go. Robin Hood Acres.

I have never been sorry that we took that money stolen from young lives and gave it back – not to the cops who stole it – but to the drug-addicted youngsters they stole it from, all those skinny kids with hungry eyes. After two months in the country, two months learning to listen to each other and themselves, skin changes, eyes fill, and these walking dead begin to laugh, to cry, to love again. Here at Robin Hood Acres, everyone has their own bed and young parents even have their own room with windows looking out onto the river. Nice to wake to birds singing in the trees.

We have an orchard, an organic garden, a pier for fishing, great lawns perfect for stargazing on new moon nights. I watch them playing ball on that lawn, and think, see, life doesn't need to be so hard. I think that and so do they. Life is beautiful. Take away the drugs and these kids are dynamos. I just try to stay out of their way, let them discover what they need to know, what they want to do. I am amazed how many stay in the community after outgrowing Robin Hood Acres, leaving this safe place where they can shake their dependency on drugs and heal. They stay, open barbershops, found libraries and schools. One couple even opened a theatre.

Our community is growing. Our little village is no longer a dying town where no one stayed after the age of eighteen. This little backwoods town is now alive with caring young people. But, don't get me wrong, there are still plenty of rocking chairs around town where the elders sit and sway. Even on our rickety porch rocking chairs sit side by side. Here, young mothers can sit and nurse their babies, chatting with one another and breathing the sweet aroma of the blooming jasmine that travels to the rafters of the porch. Small songbirds nest there amongst the dark green leaves and delicate white flowers.

More than once I have seen a young mother with her new baby asleep on her lap, her thumb pressed into the smooth curve of an eggshell, dropped from a nest.

Kali has no clothes

The day Mark left, Sally went for a long walk on the trail that hugged the cliffs overlooking Pauoa valley. She left the dogs in the backyard. Of course, they would have loved to tag along, romp on ahead as determined explorers of damp pig trails to the left or the right of trail, but she needed to be alone. She didn't want to be constantly calling them back, making sure they didn't go chasing after some caffeine hungry pig snuffling about under the coffee trees, and she certainly didn't want to have them pulling her along slippery trails at the ends of leashes. The woods were for her solitary musings today. She guessed she would probably be alone. Even though these trails were so close to downtown Honolulu, some days she hiked for hours, seeing no one, walking until the city completely disappeared into a thicket of trees murmuring songs from centuries she never knew. She hoped this would be one of those days.

She wanted to be alone with the forest, to sit for as long as she needed be silent, wait until the forest birds approached. She especially hoped to see Sharma thrushes. She knew if she whistled in imitation of the thrush's four note whistle, the bird would come ever closer until finally it would find a perch on a branch overhanging the trail, tipping its head to one side. Then, if she were lucky, the curious bird might offer her a full-throated song. It happened rarely, but the avocadoes were so very ripe, the guavas juicy and falling to the ground, any bird might be feeling the world a bountiful place, ripe with song. She laughed at such a ridiculous notion. Here she was again, defining the parameters of the bird world, a world as foreign to her as were the high mountain peaks of Tibet. She supposed that after Mark took off on his bicycle for the last time this morning, she was feeling soggy, more sentimental than rational, a bit blurred around the edges. Better to be with trees than people today. She didn't want to end up sobbing on some stranger's shoulder. Here she could use her toe to write *miss you* in the mud and then stub it out with her heel. No one would be the wiser.

Mark wasn't coming back. She knew that, but she wasn't even sure she wanted him to return. Yesterday, maybe, but today? They'd had their adventures, and there had been something like love between them. She had thought it love, he had called it love, but really she knew she didn't know much about love. How could she? Bouncing as she had from one foster home to the next, always trying to please, trying desperately to convince one mother after another to whisper *I love you*. Once, she tried to sort it out with a therapist, but that effort hadn't yielded much. Not much of use anyway. All she discovered was that her memory played tricks on her.

Mrs. Brown's face migrated to Auntie Matty's body, Aunty Matty's smile found its way to Uncle Jack's face. She no longer knew who said what, who yelled, who cajoled, who laughed, or who was just stubbornly silent twenty-four hours a day. The mother who roamed about her brain beating on her heart looked suspiciously like Kali, goddess of destruction and creation, with multiple heads and more arms than she could count. Even that was wrong. Kali only had four arms, or so she thought. Her Mama Kali didn't even have a necklace of skulls. Instead she wore a paper plumeria lei, dyed pink. But no matter. The Kali who had taken up residence in her brain as her very own substitute mama whispered *I love you* over and over again. That was enough for her.

Sally wasn't even sure she had heard anyone other than her imagined Mama Kali say *I love you* to her until Mark had whispered it to her that first night they had stayed behind in the painting studio long after class was through. That night they had talked and talked and talked, and he said *I love you* more than once. She believed him, but now when she closed her eyes and thought about love, it's wasn't Mark's face she saw. It was that same wild grinning Kali with both feet off the ground, at least one hand held high, grasping a severed head by its hair, her hair, her head, no doubt. The only demon she knew. The only love. The first foster home she remembered and the one where she stayed the longest was with Aunt Matty. Sally guessed the Kali image came from her. Matty had stretched canvas over the walls of her living room, and for the three years Sally slept in the tiny bedroom in the back, Matty was busily painting images of Kali on those canvas-lined walls. As soon as she finished one painting, she would paint it out and begin again. When the surface grew too heavy to accept more paint, Matty would strip the canvas from the wall, sand off any excess paint, and two days later, staple up a brand-new freshly gessoed canvas.

Sally never did understand what qualified Matty as a foster mother. She lived alone and never left the apartment expect to run down to the corner store for dry noodles and bottled tomato sauce, the only hot food they ate. Other than that rather dubious spaghetti (no mushrooms, no garlic, no bread), they survived on peanut butter, usually with no jelly. No milk. They drank water or green tea. Sally hadn't minded. Matty talked with her, explained things no one else explained. All that explaining, all that creating, seemed like love to Sally. Later when Sally was trying to figure out the love thing with her state approved therapist, she had tried to find Matty. She'd gone to Social Services and inquired, but of course, the folks who manned the desk were good little guard dogs. They smiled patiently at Sally, retreated to the back room, and came back to tell her that Matty Easterling was no longer in their employ, that she had finally become too ill to care for children, but during her tenure as a foster Mom she had received only the most glowing of reports, a statement Sally really didn't believe, and the plastic smile glued the clerk's face suggested that she didn't believe it either but that she intended to say no more. Smiles made good masks.

Sally remembered the day the neatly dressed social worker had dropped in unannounced a couple of days before Christmas. Sally had been home and opened the door, invited the woman in, offered to take her coat and then shepherded her into the living room where Matty was sitting on the floor, adding drips of black paint to an electric blue puddle that half-filled a cat food tin. She was wearing her white painter's overalls, splattered with more colors than blue-black, torn at both knees, with one strap held in place by a large safety pin. She was not wearing a shirt or a bra. Two half-finished paintings of Kali as her most ferocious self dominated the living room, empty of furniture except for a three-legged stool acting as a stand for a very real human skull. Matty had explained to Sally that she needed the skull as reference, to make sure she painted imagery that was true to life. That was all.

She had also tried to explain to Sally using the simplest of words that Kali was not a demon. Kali, she said, was completely misunderstood in the west. Few knew her as the dancer of creation and destruction, turning circles at the edge of things. Again and again, with her paintbrush tucked behind her ear, Matty repeated her mantra, Kali's teaching. And then translated it to words Sally could understand. Anything that dies signals a new beginning, she said. Creation isn't linear; knowledge doesn't move from A to B to Z. It is not a logical progression. It spirals, spinning in and out, reaching the furthest edges of the universe and then coiling back in to the piko, the source. Kali is that spiraling of knowledge. She is ultimate reality, the astonishing light of truth, incapable of being covered, clothed or disguised.

When Matty learned that Sally was studying Greek mythology in school, she told Sally that if she wanted to understand Kali, she might consider how Athena, goddess of wisdom, was born from the head of Zeus. She had tapped twice and then cracked his thick skull before stepping on out. Kali was also a goddess of wisdom, and she too was born from a forehead, but the forehead she cracked out of belonged to a great Goddess, Durga, the slayer of Demons. Those fifty skulls draped about her neck? One skull for every letter of the Sanskrit alphabet. All of human knowledge draped about her neck. The severed head in her hand? That was ignorance cut away by the razor sharp blade of wisdom. Both Athena and Kali were mother goddesses, sources not only of life and fertility but also of wisdom and knowledge. The comparison stopped there. Athena belonged to a male dominated hierarchy. Kali was linked to a great goddess. Athena's body was cloaked; Kali's was not.

Kali's nakedness suggests that she is freed of illusion, Matty said. She is the possessor of wisdom so brilliant, so vast, it is capable of burning away any and all shades of ignorance. She conceals nothing. As a goddess of war, Athena, on the other hand, is a master of disguise. She first disguises herself so that she might meet Odysseus, lying to him, telling him that his wife Penelope remarried (as he was believed dead), and then when Odysseus refuses to believe her, she teaches him the art of deception so that he might return as an elderly beggar to win back the favors of his beloved Penelope. Athena's wisdom is that of subterfuge and skillful prevarication, but Kali's wisdom is that of naked truth. Kali, Matty said, is *nirguna,* beyond all form and any ideas of quality. No hierarchy in Kali's web of wisdom. Athena's father, Zeus, had swallowed her Mother, Metis, whose name means simply "wisdom," because he had been told that her child would surpass him in power and wisdom. He jealously guarded his own authority. Athena's wisdom reinforces the hierarchical systems of the west. Kali's wisdom suggests that wisdom – true wisdom – is freed of system or form. Matty had asked Sally to memorize this, and she guessed she had because she still remembered it today.

Sally had tried to explain all of this to the petite young woman with her alligator skin briefcase and her lacquered blond hair, but little Miss Official took one look at Matty with her disheveled hair (very reminiscent of Kali's hair) and her paint streaked arms and gasped. When she saw the skull, it was all she could do to stammer out *Is that real?* When Matty solemnly nodded, she put her gloved hand on Sally's upper arm and dragged her into the hall, told her *STAY,* barked it out just as if she, Sally that is, was a dog, then went back in and slammed the door shut. Sally had sat down on the stairs, listened to loud voices and then silence. She remembered worrying about Matty and feeling cold. That's all. When the social worker finally came out into the hall, she had Sally's coat in one hand and her suitcase in the other.

After Matty, Sally never stayed more than three months in any foster home. Sally couldn't imagine that little Christmas scene hadn't been carefully transcribed into triplicate and stapled to Matty's file, but she supposed some sort of wisdom kept the officials from telling her the real truth about what had happened to her Auntie Matty. Athenian wisdom, no doubt, the art of concealment. Kali would have told her. Sally was certain of that.

By now Sally had been walking for more than an hour. She had left the cliffs behind, making her way down into the back of the valley where the tree roots tangled well above ground in a vast spider maze that required her full attention to get from one side to the other. Earlier, it had rained heavily. Even now a fine misting rain left her skin pleasantly damp, but the mud beneath the exposed roots was slick and the roots themselves slippery. Here it was easy to fall and end with scraped knees or worse. She picked her way across, wondering as she always did when she came to this section of the trail, if it might be better to turn back, especially as the rain was falling faster now, and she was starting to feel wet instead of glowingly damp, but there was no turning back. Early this morning, she had decided that she was going to walk all the way to the waterfall and then hightail it down that tourist highway of a trail at the back of Manoa Valley, and she intended to do just that.

If she turned back now, she would have to walk all the way down Tantalus, past the house where Mark had moved with sharp-nosed Nora. She would have to keep her eyes fixed on the far side of the road, keep herself from letting them drift over to the wide front window of the house with its fern-green linen curtains, open during the day but drawn tight at night, closed over Mark's painting of Kali. It was that painting that had brought them together when they were both art students at the Academy. It had startled her, and when he reiterated everything that Matty had told her – at least everything she remembered – she trusted him. In retrospect, she supposed she should have asked him – ever so politely – if he believed any of what he was telling her. When he unhooked the painting from the wall of their apartment and tied it to the back of his bike, she knew he was gone for good. He refused to tell her where he was going, but it hadn't taken Sally too long to find out his whereabouts. Obviously, Mark hadn't yet figured out that Kali can't be concealed behind drapes.

If she stayed on the trail, she would be in the back of Manoa just as the sun was slumping back behind the ridge. She'd catch the bus back into town, pick up some sesame noodles at the corner café and eat on her tiny little balcony overlooking one of the filthiest alleys she had ever seen. Tomorrow, she'd stretch canvas on the living room wall.

Wardrobe

I emptied all my closets and sorted through the drawers in my bedroom. Clothes are everywhere – hanging from the backs of doors, scattered across the floor, piled so high on the bed that it is entirely possible that when I get to the bottom of the pile some neighbor kid might just pop out and yell, "Surprise!" The pile seems way too high to be simply clothes, folded or not. I could plant a flag on it and found my own island nation.

How in the world did I come to have so many clothes and whatever made me feel I needed them? It's a mystery but one that I have very very little interest in figuring out. Not now anyway. All I need to do is sort them, get them ready for recycling, sale, or donating. As much as I need money, I really don't think there's enough time for a sale. It's off to the Goodwill with Cousin Susie's beautiful satin shoes that she gave me to wear to that silly ga-ga-gag-me-with-a-spoon-gala staged by her company last March, and it's away to Salvation Arm with the fourteen pairs of ski boots "acquired" over the years in the hope that invitations to Tahoe, or better yet St Moritz, would pile up on my bedside table. One pair is even lined with mink, bought to attract some rich bachelor with a foot fetish, I suppose. And those silver high-heels. What *was* I thinking? Did I really think that I would attend some late night high-rise party with gallons of champagne and acres of over-inflated helium balloons, trip on my way down the stairs, and then make some big fuss about being unable to find my wayward shoe before climbing into the cab barefoot with my remaining sparkling heel in hand? Did I really think some Prince Charming was going to stand at the top of the stairs, see my naked foot, and look desperately for the shoe before discovering it in the underbrush? Did I really think it was possible for some one to fall in love with the imprint of an absent foot in some silly shoe and then search me out? Had I been *that* indoctrinated by fairy tales? Goodness knows, I couldn't walk in those things, and each shoe, not each pair, cost me a week's salary.

That wasn't as bad as that full-length made-for-me-and-me-alone ostrich leather coat with its expansive leopard skin collar. I only wore that coat once and when I did, I turned heads, I can tell you that. I stand over six-foot tall and am so skinny I disappear when I turned sideways – I kid you not. A raving beauty, Georgie used to say, but that's not why folks stared. They were outraged. I'd thought it daring and exotic to have a coat made of the skins of creatures who, in any other circumstances, would have torn each other apart, a marriage of enemies, so to speak, but no one else got the joke. They thought it barbaric, and if the coat was barbaric, well, then, *obviously* so was I. Even the bellboy wouldn't carry my bag. I had to drag that over-stuffed Gucci-monogrammed knock-off piece of *trash* up to my room myself.

Oh the stuff of memories, the compost of the brain.

And what *have* we here? Oh yes, my prized collection of pure silk negligees, each hand-stitched, purportedly in Paris but really, no doubt, in some sweatshop in Thailand where crowds of nine-year-olds sat shoulder-to-shoulder plying tiny needles to make the neat little stitches the brochure advertised as "artistic" and "eminently practical." Hand-sewn silk, the salesman had told me, holds up far far better than anything sewn on a machine. He brushed the fabric on my cheek and looked so deep into my eyes I thought he would drown and then crooned in his whiskey voice a few well-chosen words about the brutality of machines.

Can you believe that I actually *fell* for that?

Of course, he never mentioned the starving orphans ruining their eyes trying to stitch black lace onto black silk undies in some backroom where there were no fans and temperatures never fell below 105 degrees Fahrenheit. Do you think I would have bought these things had I known they weren't really made by kindly French grandmothers with blue hair who wanted something to do with their afternoons but *instead* were stitched by tiny girls with stick arms who were paid two dollars a week, if that? Not on your life. Call me naïve, but I really did believe that almond-faced clerk with his pencil thin mustache. I actually thought I was helping older women live decent lives in expensive Paris.

Okay, I wasn't too smart.

All right, tell it like it is. It's not that I was just a teency eency bit naive. I was damn stupid, a total dunce, to buy that stuff in the first place, but why beat myself up? I was just a motherless girl trying to get along in a world that never much respected mothers anyway. I swear all the mothers died or disappeared in every Disney movie I saw when I was a kid, and the stepmothers were usually wicked and mean. I mean, let's talk about Cinderella, shall we? The only mother I knew who got any respect was Mother Mary, and as she apparently never had sex before giving birth, what did she know about the world of men and women?

Everybody I met tried to convince me I wasn't a worthy to be called woman unless I painted my nails, decorated my face, and dressed in fine linen and silk. Women, I learned, should try first and foremost to look pretty and smile. Don't worry about vocabulary lists, just avoid intelligent conversation. "Yes" is the only word you need to know.

Maybe if I had said "no" or, better yet, "what?" more than "yes" I wouldn't be bagging up all these barely worn "come hither" nothings. I said "yes" to the lipstick, yes to the baseball player with the cute smile, "yes" to the bartender, "yes" to the bored husband who lived down the street. I said "yes" too many times but never to that most important question that might have let me have more closets. So here I sit, sorting through the years, cataloguing the "yea", finding no "nays." So to speak.

Even when I realized I would need to go back to school, I didn't stop saying yes. I said "yes" to the registrar, "yes" to the graduate student who promised to help me study for my exams, "yes" to the professor who kept score in a private notebook stuffed in the back of his desk. I even said "yes" to the stoner custodian who promised me more coke than I could easily snort in a week.

Why on earth I decided to get a BA in Communication, I have no idea. I guess, the first drama class convinced me. I needed drama, communicating was good. Here was this cute guy, my age, standing up in front of everyone, having a great time talking about clothes, describing the reason why this particular gown or that was attractive, actually saying out-loud that bias-cut silk lay like rose petals on the hip, reminding anyone who chose to look of those even softer petals within. I was amazed. He was a *guy*, sweet looking sure, but a *guy*. Petals within? What petals? Then he started talking about cross-dressing as if it were some sort of erudite philosophy or something – all this stuff about the metaphorical space of aporia or some such thing. I just gave up and watched his dimples move about on all that lovely ebony skin. I even said "yes" to my advisor when he asked he me what I would do with my BA. I just shrugged and he said, well, any law firm in town would welcome someone like you, a good communicator who can write. Would I like to work for lawyers? I said "yes."

Lawyers? What was I thinking? Glamour, I guess. Like on TV.

Always solving problems while dressed tin the latest and the best. Ah, the glitz of the sparkle screen. The "Firm" and all that. My first day on the job I wore my hand-stitched glove leather Italian black heels – nothing too flashy – a wispy grey silk shirt with a taupe linen suit (silk lined). The only adornment – hand-made oyster shell buttons. Everything well-designed, cleanly cut.

Cleanly cut, as it turned out, by gnarled hands of amputees in Nicaragua, folks who, according to these "humanitarian" lawyers would be dead if not for the "piece-work" provided by this high-end manufacturer. Ha. I walked into that office with my heels clicking crisply on the marble floor, convinced I was off to save the world, one comma at a time. And what did I find? Hypocrisy.

I really thought I was going to be having cocktails with smart men and women, helping them find ways to help others – I actually believed that *all* lawyers, despite their irascible nastiness, ultimately worked hard to make the world a better place. Ha.

Maybe some lawyers do just that, who knows, but not these yoyos. I was just a file clerk, hired at a low wage hoping for a promotion and a raise. Ha, again. No raise, but I sure did learn a lot.

One thing I will say about clerical work – it gives you plenty of access to files. I suppose it was worth spending two years as underpaid coffee maven to learn what I learned. I suppose. I suppose my getting that job was karmic justice or some such thing, pay back for my wardrobe fetish. After all, I know they hired me for my stylish wardrobe not my degree. Somehow I managed to find a job with the very folk who were drawing up those ironclad precisely worded contracts that made it "legal" for "a major manufacturer" to hire barefoot children to work in their overseas sweatshops. And I had to make them coffee.

Just for your information, dear reader, on the advice of another group of lawyers, the publisher's lawyers, I am writing "major manufacturer" instead of the name of the company. I asked that crew (the other lawyers) with *their* Italian shoes just what I *can* say and so I will say that this "major manufacturer" makes the kind of running shoes sought after by every aspiring sports enthusiast and jogger in the USA. The things I learned. The things they learned.

They managed to use all they learned from their clients' sweatshop to recreate their own mini law-firm sweatshop. I still can't believe I worked there for six months for *free*. Internship. Ha. Always hoping that they would hire me. They finally did for $200/wk (didn't even pay my rent), but when they actually had to pay me, the job went away. They quickly found not just one intern but two, didn't need me anymore. They had it covered. They knew when those interns wore out, there were plenty more eager faces waiting in the shadows, willing to work for free, believing (quite incorrectly, of course) they would soon be indispensible. Ha. What egos. They were no more indispensible than I was.

I suppose I should sort these clothes into piles of sweatshop products and, how shall I put it, ethical clothing, but the trouble is I think it would all end up in one huge pile. I'm beginning to wonder. . . is there such a thing as ethics in clothes manufacturing? In any business? Am I to describe as ethical that "major department store" whose CEO made enough money to acquire quite an extensive art collection that was, to his credit, I suppose, donated to a "major" metropolitan museum when they advertise as ethically produced all those hip little "look-at-me-I'm-slumming" shirts? I dunno. And as for my running shoes, well, *you* know that story. What a motto. Do what? Enslave others so Americans can run in comfort and you can make billions? Oh boy. Okay, maybe "enslave" is too harsh a word; these folks *are* getting paid after all, just not a living wage, and I ask you this, can any sane person really believe that giving 'bonuses' to workers who tolerate the headaches that come from assembling shoes with toxic glue makes it right? Yup, if I start sorting now, I would just have one huge mountain of clothes bought for huge amounts of cash, all made by overseas workers working in toxic environments while living on starvation wages and dreaming of fancy cars parked in front of even fancier houses in American suburbs.

Okay, I was foolish, but really what did I know then? I was just some poor chick from the ghetto, a daughter of non-English speaking immigrant parents with stars in their eyes who convinced me that if I said "yes" to the world, the world would say "yes" to me. I had *no idea* how things "really" work. I believed the American dream – work hard and anything's possible – but these folks, manufacturers, lawyers, they *knew*. My goodness, I should have had a *clue*, for goodness sake. Nobody calls it the American "truth." It really is a *dream*, one of those fleeting fogs that fill the desperate hours of night with sparkle and grace. They *knew*. The following documents reveal

* * * * *

"That's *it*?"

Detective Thomas carefully slipped into a glassine envelope the three sheets of paper handed to him by the patrolman who had spent the last few minutes reading them aloud to all present, including those who had come to survey the room and also the tiny body curled atop a mountain of clothes.

"Where *are* the 'documents' she mentions?"

The patrolman shrugged. "Don't know. We looked, didn't find any. Just those papers scattered by the door."

"Any sign of break-in? Any sign of struggle?"

"Look for yourself, Jim. Nothing but mounds of clothes. The struggle was here and here," pointing first to his head and then to his hand flat against his chest. "That's what this scribble seems to suggest anyway, don't you think?"

Although the window's open, allowing the breezes from the harbor beyond to sift into the room, the screen was not torn. The dust on the windowsill undisturbed. Detective Thomas glanced at face of the young girl curled in the nest-like hollow atop the mountain of clothes. Brilliantly colored silk scarves are stuffed near her head at one end of the shallow indentation and for one irrational moment he thinks of a pea and the brand-new root just visible on its rounded face. Next to the bed dozens of shoeboxes tower precariously, almost reaching the ceiling. He supposed they would have to remove each lid and peer inside. He hopes to see only shoes and no dead rats, no dried spiders or worse.

Jotting a few sentences in his notebook, Detective Thomas shook his head, picked up the empty pill bottle from the floor and dropped it into a ziplock bag. Despite the phone call from homicide, it was clear this was an open and shut case. He had done his homework before driving over, checked with the girl's employer, interviewed the friend who had called 911, the landlord, anyone he thought might have something to say. The girl had been recently laid off; she was about to be evicted, and according to her friend she was so deep in debt she would never crawl out. It was tragic, yes, but didn't look like murder, looked more like the young woman just ran out of steam. After all her written statement made it all pretty clear that she had made some bad decisions, gone to work for the wrong folk, but you can't charge folks with murder if they underpay their employees.

"Can you?"

"Huh? Can I what?"

Seeing his partner's puzzled expression, Detective Thomas realized he had spoken aloud. "Oh, nothing. I was just thinking about law, ethics, murder. That was some helluva letter she wrote."

"Yeah, I suppose, more like a letter to the editor than a suicide note. Whadya think, Jim? Shall we close the case?"

Detective Thomas allowed his eyes to roam the room again, passing over the stacks of books near the bed, the single potted plant in the corner with its drooping leaves. He walked again to the bathroom door, looked again at the tiny bathroom window, the closed vent, the towel on the floor. He checked again the door for any signs of forced entry but found nothing out of place other than a tiny chip high up on the door jam. He turned the doormat over, nothing but ordinary dirt, accumulated over days.

"Case closed. Suicide." Jim looked down at his own scuffed shoes, union made. "Tell the Goodwill to send someone over for the clothes. It's the least we can do."

Borderline

Colin hesitated on the last step of the stairs leading to the beach. Even in the dim dawn light he could see that last night the sea had risen higher than usual at high tide. This sand was smoothed to a fine polish sparking blue and green neon under the light of the full moon. His would be the first footprint on the beach, but he wasn't sure he wanted that responsibility. It was easy to walk with delicacy and grace on the beach when it was rumpled by dozens of feet, but when his foot was the first to dent that silvered plane, he felt somehow awkward and boorish, too heavy. It made him feel like a misplaced comma or an unnecessary semi-colon, and he had enough of those at work. He didn't need to be one.

The moon was struggling between pale and extravagant, slipping ever so slowly toward the clouds that always nestled at the horizon, and for the first time, Colin noticed a jerkiness to the moon's descent, almost as if he were watching a poorly-made animated film. It couldn't be that the earth itself was stuttering. It had to be his eyes. He lifted his hand and ran his fingers over the top of his skull, letting his fingers drift through his hair until his palm rested on the back of his neck. He rubbed his thumb along his shoulder bone. Last night, annoyed by the electronic buzzing of the aging appliances in the house, he had grabbed his quilts, walked to the far edge of the lawn beside the naupaka hedge and bedded down, tossed and turned as the damp burrowed deep into his back, knotting his muscles and dulling his joints. He had wanted to be under the stars, but the ground had been too hard and the moon too bright. He hadn't slept well.

Editing online was beginning to take its toll. This morning when he woke, groggy from a dream that involved houses rocking uneasily on a moving sea and clouds made of something that looked suspiciously like polyester batting, he felt as if his blood was becoming electrified, his bones morphing into tangled warps of URLs. He stumbled back to his bed, slept for a few minutes only, and when he opened his eyes, everything in the room – the bedstead, the bureau, his narrow desk – sparked haloes of electric blue light that looked suspiciously like the afterglow of a computer, recently silenced.

Colin had lurched from bed, shaking his arms rapidly, hoping to shed some if not all the electric surge, but had only ended feeling limp, drained of energy. He needed to jog on the beach away from any electricity, inside moonlight, but now he couldn't even set his foot on the sand. He was like Dr. Doolittle's Pushmepullyou, desire pitted against something that felt uncomfortably like an overprotective mother, keeping him not from danger but from the world. One said go and the other said stay. He could neither move at speed nor stay comfortably at rest, staring at the fading river of stars overhead. He was mired in muck. Or buried in dust.

When he breathed, he tasted sea foam, but when he closed his eyes, he saw the sun suspended in the sky near its zenith, perfectly round and dully silver, almost white, a noonday moon trapped in a sky exhausted by dust. When he had returned after that semester of teaching in West Africa, he was grateful to find his feet on familiar ground again, glad to smell the air as flushed with rain and flowers instead of oil and dust, but when that initial surge of joy faded, he had felt erased. Now, all he heard were echoes.

Before him the sea stretched to the horizon, but every step he took pulled him backwards into that small cramped room on the edge of the Sahel. It wasn't the palm trees he heard, it wasn't the waves. It was Anna's soft voice as she stood as she so often did at the end of the workday, her back to him, fingers drumming on the hard surface of her desk, every muscle in her body stretched into the south bent wind pulling away, looking for entry to the hurricane track across western seas.

"Now, there's no phone."

Refusing to turn around, Anna tapped the window glass.

"No internet. Our car's dead, and now no phone."

Outside yellowed fields and distant mountains came and went behind a film of thick blowing dust and thin blue smoke, rising from trash fires burning in fields closer to town. Harmattan, when desert winds picked up as much of the Sahara as possible and flung it at the cracked landscape, had already lasted longer than anyone wanted it to but if the winds were any indication, it would continue. And continue. Outside, close to the road that he supposed had once been neatly paved but was now a maze of potholes, a skinny goat with a swollen belly put one leg against the gnarled stump of the one bush left with green leaves and heaved its frail body to the vertical, stretching its neck to reach the last remaining leaves that dangled within reach. Two newborns huddled motionless nearby, their ragged coats thick with sulphur-yellow dust.

"Great," Anna placed her palm flat against the windowpane. "Can't even call someone to fix it. No one to call."

At that moment, as if in response to the hand flat on glass, the electricity failed with its usual suddenness. The overhead lights blacked out; the AC shut down, and in the dim light of Harmattan, shadow blurred. Anna turned and faced Colin, twisting her face into a grimace that resembled the most ferocious of the masks they had bought last week from the man who once a week drove to town from the bush, his beat-up station wagon packed with dirt encrusted carvings and an occasional mask. She sat down suddenly and heavily, both elbows balanced on the edge of her desk, both hands spread with open fingers across her face.

Illuminated by the strange yellow light of Harmattan, with her eyes held wide, pale skin stretched over prominent cheekbones, she morphed from mask to moth caught in the light of her own spider web hands. She sat unmoving for more time than was necessary, not blinking, even as Colin reached his hand across the desk to twine his fingers gently on hers.

"Anna."

Colin took his hand from hers and reached behind him, lifting a ripe and very red tomato from the shelf holding his battered copies of Dickens. "Anna, have you eaten anything, anything at all today? Anything? Anything at all...how about...this..."

Oddly, decent tomatoes were not nearly so difficult to find in April here in this region as they were in the States. Tomatoes grew rapidly in the sandy hot soils at the edge of the Sahel, despite the dust and the blowing plastic bags masquerading as crows, but there was little time to eat between classes. Both Colin and Anna found that the frequent electricity outages and unreliable internet meant that they had to use every available minute of electricity to finish the computer work required for their computer-driven classes and for their own research. Why they were expected to teach computer skills and computer driven classes in a locale with spotty electricity had never been explained. Fortunately the computer geniuses who spoke only Russian and skulked around in the lab knew how to fix Apple power cords, which blew out as frequently as the electricity failed. Outages were preceded by electrical surges of gargantuan dimensions.

They frequently ate only in the dark at their desks after the electricity, the internet, or both had failed. After that first week of absurdly hoping that promised technology would magically appear, they had found a way to finish all that needed to be finished – work like demons on fire when the electricity flowed easily and eat and maybe sleep when it surged wildly and failed. Use failure to your advantage, Colin had said, and Anna had laughed.

Then. Now, it no longer seemed funny.

Tomatoes and potatoes were two of the foods that Colin identified as local "survival" foods – both had enough sugar and starch to sustain and even nourish the body – but Anna rarely ate anything except dried blueberries and salted salmon brought from home. Not such a bad diet, he guessed, but one that required open connections to what he now called "the outside world," and three months into the semester both knew that depending on those connections was a bit like believing one could tie a rope around a shark and be dragged from one continent to another. Not bloody likely.

"Anna," Colin spoke in a whisper. "It'll get better; our car will be fixed. We *will* have electricity, food, water. If I'm certain anything, I'm certain of this: We *will* survive."

"Survive??" Anna dropped her hands from her face. She glared at him. "Do you think this is about survival?? I'm trying to teach here, but how can I? Every piece of equipment in my lab doesn't work. The last one they brought in, they plugged into the bad outlet – even though I *told* them not to – and the damn thing fried *instantly*. $3000 down the tubes, and do you really think they'll buy another?? No way. Every sample in the freezer thawed to instant mush. Worthless. I can't teach scientific practice. All I can do is speak of history, talk about Marie Curie and the conditions she endured, but so what?? What good is that? You too can suffer? So?? This isn't a University. It's a joke."

The goat across the way had given up trying to nibble the two remaining green leaves of the bush and was now trying to cross the road with the two babies close at her heels. No sooner was she on the road when a car bounced by, and the goat flung her head to one side, stepping suddenly backwards into the ditch.

"Oh, those babies!" Colin gasped.

"What the HELL are you talking about, Colin? What babies? We don't have any babies. If you mean my samples, they're not babies – just frozen spiders and a few strange beetles." Anna slammed her hand into the desk. "Get REAL, Colin, get out if your poetic haze for once and SEE what is going on around here."

"Oh, sorry. I was watching the goats."

"The goats, the goats, why the HELL are you always talking about goats? Who CARES about the goats? Don't you SEE what is going on in this zone??" Anna picked up her water bottle and drained the last of the water into her mouth. "No electricity. No car. No internet. No water. No education. No education, no future. No future for democratic thinking anyway. Goats, Colin? Get real."

Anna heaved her empty water bottle at the wall above his head. "Goats can take care of themselves."

The window shivered as the winds grew stronger, spitting fine grains of sand against the glass, turning the everyday fragile music to raucous cacophony. The steady hiss of wires brushed against a snare drum, the lapsed breathing of the constant trash fires burning in the barren lot next door . . . sounds that ordinarily awakened them at dawn, put them to sleep at night . . . now buried beneath wilder rising winds. Colin had never before spent days and then months in a region where the air made noise without the help of even with the slightest of breezes. Daily, the air hummed loudly, so when Harmattan arrived, it became symphonic.

Every afternoon, as they waited for the bus at 5:15, the air scratched across their skin, rasping like some anemic ghost with more fingernails than anyone could count. When they walked the last half-mile from the road to the housing compound, they could hear the air seething through the burning piles of trash on either side of the dirt track leading to locked gate that separated their squat cinderblock house from the surrounding mud huts with their thatched roofs. When that locked gate opened, the air hissed; when it closed, it belched. Colin sometimes imagined that the goats survived by nibbling that breathing sighing air, skinning it down to its ashy marrow. Until it all blew away, heading off to hurricane alley.

"The goats are starving, Anna."

"And, so, Colin, are the *people*. You, Colin, are a fool. This, my friend, is where the desert creeps in, steals every last bit of food."

Anna raised her hand and, like a magician passed it over the collapsing bookshelves, the broken window, the barren drying landscape outside with its two dead trees and one bush finally most recently stripped of leaves and covered with yellow dust. If looks could kill, the daggers Anna sent his direction would have left him skewered to the wall, gasping for breath and unable to make the nine hour journey north to the airport the following month when he decided he had breathed enough solid air to last a lifetime.

When he first arrived, he had been so convinced that he would be able to "contribute." The Great White Hope. Anna was right.

He was a fool.

He had wanted to believe that his impassioned lectures about Wordsworth might convince his students, more at home with violence, to slow down and appreciate their world, but when he looked about he saw no drifting bouts of pretty, only flocks of black plastic bags, dead crows snagged on dead tree branches.

One late afternoon, he had tired of waiting for the bus and walked the four miles home, crossing vast fields that perhaps had once nurtured crops but now served as garbage dumps for acres and acres of plastic packaging. One use, he thought, for Nigerian oil. Make more plastic bags, convince everyone that those black plastic bags snagged in trees are better than birds. Under one of those trees, dripping black plastic, the middle of a field of dead and dying grass crusted black from trash piles recently burned, he found a single mound of sweet potatoes, dark green leaves damp from a recent watering and alive with fragile white flowers. Each bloom opened to the swirling spirals of blue smoke rising to the yellowed sky. He had stood there for what seemed to be hours, watching as the pristine white petals blued with the failing light as the flower's purple center deepened into the dusk. That flower, he decided, was the most beautiful flower on earth. It took his breath but offered him a way to soar above the smoke and breathe instead the exhalations of stars.

He had walked home in the dark with nothing to light his way except the thin red lines of the burning crowns of trash heaps and then wrote the first poem he had been able to write since arriving. The next day, he spent some minutes at the beginning of each class describing his walk and what he had found in the middle of that field on fire. His tale had triggered an impassioned discussion about beauty and the nature of beauty. Was it similitude? Was it startling contrast? He left the question unanswered and asked his students to go home and to return with written descriptions of something beautiful.

Colin had not been surprised by the essays about flowers or starry skies written on perfumed paper, but he had been amazed by the essays describing the beauty of sharpened blades, gun barrels glinting in the sun. He was stunned into silence by two essays describing the beauty of slaughter, including descriptions of blood spilling into rivers, filling dry wells, sinking hearts. When he had handed the goriest yet the best written essay back to the young man who had written about the exquisite beauty of blood congealing on sand, he had asked him why anyone would want to take another's life, why anyone would want to hack a body to pieces. The young man stepped closer and stared at Colin's quizzical face. He hadn't laughed or smirked or sneered. He just grabbed his essay with both hands and said as loudly and as cleanly as possible *because it's fun.* He paused, not for dramatic effect, but because he seemed genuinely unsure what he would say next. Then he repeated himself *because it's fun.* Colin knew he meant every word.

Now, nine thousand miles away, under the wash of the Milky Way with the wind gently lifting the fronds of the palm trees next to a beach wet with waves and glitterstruck with moon, Colin could not step onto the sand.

Dear Killer Boy

I'm writing by the light of the moon and inside a fierce wind rushing out of the valley mouth and kicking up the sand on the beach. I figure must be some kind of wild storm on the other side of the island if a wind this strong is slamming over the mountains and rushing out to sea with such force. It's cold – cold enough for heavy sweaters and socks, and, I suppose, if it's only cold enough for sweaters and socks that might seem warm to those who are battling snow in the dark lands of the north but here in the Pacific we don't appreciate cold winds even if sometimes we expect them especially at this time of year, which is November, but I am getting ahead of myself and I'm running out of breath.

The fact of the matter is I don't have a sweater and I sure as hell don't have socks. I've been out here on this end of the island living in a tent on the beach for the last six months or so and nobody knows I'm here. I mean nobody who counts for nothing, like my sergeant, that gung-ho platoon leader, who couldn't shut up about how many Iraqis he killed and how many more he intended to kill. That's *you*, killer boy. I got so sick and tired of listening to all that crap running out of your mouth that I just packed my gear and left the day before we were scheduled to leave for Iraq. I decided I'd had enough. I wasn't going to kill anyone.

Wow, that was one helluva a gust of wind. Glad I have my tent tethered with boulders not just rocks. Smart move, Jerrycan, smart move. As you might guess, that's not my real name. After all, I'm officially AWOL, gone fishin', out to lunch, outta town. But that's what I call myself. Not like "jerrycan," the thing, but like "jerrycan" with a verb, jerry can do, jerry can go, and jerry did go. Wasn't that hard actually. I went to the lock-up, used the key we got (and I won't tell you how), took what army issue hardware I could carry, not much but some. A couple of M-16s, a box of bullets, stuffed the whole lot in my handy-dandy black garbage bag and then walked out behind the barracks, way out into those dry scratchy weeds. I had a shovel and meant to dig a deep hole, throw all that junk down the hole and bury it, but I got lucky.

Somewhere out back, somewhere we never went, not as a team anyway, I stumbled over what was either an old bore hole or one of those lava tubes my buddy Keanu was always talking about. I threw some rocks down inside. I never heard one hit bottom so I began to throw the ammo in, bullet by bullet, but don't worry. I made sure it wouldn't explode. I dipped each bullet into this gallon can of roofing tar I'd lugged out with me, coated each one in sticky goo and then tossed it down. I suppose that's not very ecological but what's better, live ammo or dead ammo? I always say the only good bullet is a dead bullet.

I'll say this too. I never heard any explosions when I tossed those bullets down the hole even though they must have fallen far enough to pick up quality speed, as we say, so I suppose my little plan worked. After I had "unburdened" myself – ha ha – down the hole, let that load drop down on top of all those little death machines, I sat for a while on this huge lava rock worn as smooth as the palm of my hand and took apart the M-16s. When they were in pieces – some tiny, some not so tiny – I went back to base and walked around, putting one or two pieces in every garbage can I saw. The dumpster outside the officers' mess hall got the ever-so-special non-replaceable trigger mechanisms, those indispensible pieces of shit now neatly disposed under acres of kitchen trash. I waited until the kitchen crew started up the path with their barrels of potato peelings, carrot tops, fish guts, and yesterday's lunch. As soon as they were marching up the hill, I tipped my garbage sack into the dumpster, clickety-clack. You want those triggers back? Go fishing, Killer Boy.

Then, I found my civvies – the jeans and t-shirts I had brought with me from home – and stuffed them in another plastic garbage sack. But no socks. No sweater. The minute the plane set down in Honolulu, I took my socks off and stuffed them in that Agriculture Amnesty bin, joking with my buddy Steve that Hawai'i's agriculture boys would have some fun sorting out Missouri's fleas. I didn't figure I'd be needing any socks in Hawai`i. After all, ain't this place Paradise?

Hey, hey, hey, I know what you're doing, marking down the names of my buddies, noting my home state, figuring that's how you'll find me, but give it up, killer boy. Do you *really* think I would put *real* info like *that* in a note like *this*? No way. Keanu? Not his name. Not even close. Steve? Not his name. He answers to some other moniker. Missouri? Never been there, but I *am* mainland. Yup, me and how many other thousands. Go figure. You'll just have to guess.

I can *see* you rolling your eyes, muttering to that guy with the stone chin and all those stars and bars decorating his chest that I must be really dumb, that I somehow forgot all you have to do is check out who left, who disappeared. Yeah, you go ahead and do that, killer boy, but what you and I both know is that the *whole platoon* took off. Yeah, yeah, I'm not just a lonely renegade fed up with the kill-kill-kill mentality of the US Army. We were *all* fed up and we planned this mass exit. Together, killer boy. A joint effort.

Took us months and you know the funny thing is, our little plan actually worked. Nothing like a good old patriotic holiday like the Fourth of July to provide cover for departure. Nothing like "bombs exploding in air" to shield a meltdown. You can drag me out of my flimsy tent, killer boy, and shine your high voltage lights in my eyes, pour water down my throat, but you won't get more from me than I'm telling you here. I really don't know where the other guys went. They just melted off into the night. Oh say can you see. The thing is nobody did see. Hell, they haven't been seeing anything for a while, a good long while. Born on the Fourth of July. That's me. Reborn anyway.

I'd mouthed off to the sergeant that morning so I was on garbage duty, which was fine with me, made the garbage bag for my clothes a-okay. I never made it down to the festivities, just walked off base and hopped the bus to Wai`anae. Been here ever since. Maybe. You can look but you won't find me. Cause maybe I'm just not here. Or *there*. Or anywhere. That's okay. You can just stop looking for me. I'm not looking for trouble. Most likely, you *have* stopped looking for those of us who melted away on that Fourth of July. Ya see, killer boy, you know and I know, the guys with the stars and the bars don't want the American public to know that a whole platoon went AWOL, not good publicity for their nasty little war games. Might damage morale and all that.

So they're keeping the whole thing under cover, but I know our plan worked. We can all feel good about doing our bit for our country, staying away from war. We're working for our country, not the shoot 'em up country, but our people country, mothers and babies, gardens and chickens. I hear from some of my buds now and again. They're here there and everywhere, melting back into the stewpot, I guess.

Most just checked out of Hawai`i, went down to the docks and boarded yachts waiting in the dark. You'd be surprised, killer boy, how many folks are not gun-ho yeah-yeah for war, how many are actually eager to help soldiers escape the killing road. Just like way back in the days of Vietnam, a bunch went to Canada, but this time, folks, we melt-aways are melting back in. I can tell you SK's working in his cousin's day care center somewhere in the middle of Nebraska. TJ's paving roads in NJ, and KP's here with me. We're building a fishing business. Better than war business.

Yeah, Vietnam, Canada, the South Seas. My dad was a Vietnam vet so you might say I never really knew him. I mean, he tried to be good father and all that. On his good days, when there was light in his eyes, he took me to ball games, taught me how to fish, how to build a fire that would light with one match, but usually he was absent somehow. At least that's what I remember.

He died when I was twelve, and I know that memory is sometimes a curtain covering the stage so don't quote me, killer boy. Can't tell how much of this is 100% accurate but I do know that the main points are. In the winter, Dad sat for hours staring through the window at nothing but snow spiraling in the porch light. Odd. It's not that the never-ending snow spirals weren't fascinating. They were. One night, I sat and watched them for a while with him. I let my mind fall into the swirling snow until I was a universe forming. It was awesome.

After that night I had a great deal more respect for snow staring, but I couldn't tell him that. Well, I might have, but he might not have answered. Most days, he never said a word. One January afternoon when the sun was glaring off the piled snow, my sister climbed in his lap but he didn't even put his arm around her. He just sat there staring. I heard my Mom talking on the phone with her sister the next day. She called Dad a "living monument to war," said he should be installed in D.C. instead of that polished black slab carved with all those names. Nothing polished about veterans of war, she said. Hers, she said, was filled with holes. I guess, in the end, it was the polish of that monument that shattered his own bronze exterior, let his heart out, left him dead.

Every year in July – always July – he would take to the road. Usually he drove north. Mom told us he needed time "alone" (as if he was never alone in our house) to think. She tried to explain to us about the war without being too graphic, but I got the picture. Thatched roofs on fire, kids running down dirt roads with flames on their backs, mothers dead with babies bleeding and mewling in their arms. She said Dad being there, seeing all that, *that* had made him silent. All that death was still inside his heart, that's what she said, and sometimes he just needed to go deep into the woods and let it all out.

When I asked her why he didn't just go into the backyard and yell at the pine trees, she laid her hand on my cheek and said in that soft musical voice of hers, almost like humming it was, that she didn't know, but she knew he couldn't. He couldn't cry here in his home in front of her in front of us. Here he had to be strong, a monument to war, steel and stone.

Well, he's not here now. And I miss him. I miss my Mom. I miss her hand on my cheek. I really wish I had known my Dad better, really wish I had better memories than him staring out at snow. Sometimes, late at night when me and the guys are sitting down by the surf, telling stories, I think I see Dad, sitting out there, cross-legged on the waves looking at me with those empty eyes. I know he wants to tell me something. I like to think he's glad I threw those bullets down that hole, glad I'm dodging rogue waves rather than rogue bullets, glad I'm exploding with love not hate.

I'm getting ahead of myself again or falling behind, can't tell which. Anyway, one July Dad threw his duffle into our broken down Camaro, and we all knew right away he was off on one of his "fishing" trips. When the car pulled out, I kicked the porch rail so hard I think I jarred it loose. I was mad. More than mad. I was furious.

Dad's little excursions always upset our household, but this summer both my older sister and my Mom had jobs and I was the star pitcher on my Little League team. My sister was working at the Dairy Queen about four miles down the road and Mom had a job right near the baseball diamond at the other end of town. I told my sis that she could use my bike to get back and forth from work, that I would drive to the ball field with Mom and come home when she finished work. It was a good plan, and I felt like a real grown-up thinking it up, especially the part about the bike. The plan was working. At first, our days were seamless, but when Dad powered up the Camaro and took off in a cloud of smoke, I knew what it meant.

Yeah, sure, Dad would be gone for a few weeks, but we were used to that. After all, like I said, he was more absent than present most if the time. Actually, truthfully, our house got livelier when Dad took to the woods. We all laughed more, or so it seemed. Then, anyway. The problem was that he took the car. Our only car. Mom and I would have to be on the bus, and the bus route required changing buses midstream, then waiting for what always seemed to be an hour for another broken-down bus to come chugging up the road. My practice schedule would be shot to hell. As far as my pea-brain knew, those taillights turning the corner, heading to the highway, signaled the end of my illustrious pitching career in the majors. I was so pissed, I put my fist through the screen door, and I have been swimming through that hole ever since.

Dad never came home from that fishing trip. He didn't get lost in the woods or blown away by the tornado that set down just a few miles away from his fishing camp that week. He never went to the woods. He drove instead to D.C. and got lost in the shadows of another forest thousands of miles away, a rainforest on fire, and I can tell you this, the tornado that hurled him into the ground was on no one's radar screen. What we learned later was that Dad had gone to the Vietnam Memorial, that slick polished stone so dark it swallows any reflection, and made rubbings of the neatly carved names of his buddies killed in the war. Then, he went back to the motel and wrote the details of their deaths on tiny slips of paper that he sewed to the rice paper rubbing with pieces of red cotton thread. That's the part that I can't seem to forget. It still lives in my heart – Dad's fingers pulling a needle and thread through the thick rice paper, attaching each tiny tab, all those little flags of life fluttering on that paper tomb. Markers.

Imagine *this*. The police actually rolled the rice paper screen up and presented to my mother – a sacred testament of war, more commandments than ten – but by then, it was so covered with blood that we really couldn't read most of the names or any of details of death. Those little warning flags were glommed one to another. Blood brothers still, I guess. After Dad fleshed out those names with details of life and death, he took his hunting rifle out of his duffle bag, rigged up a way to pull the trigger, put the muzzle in his mouth and blew his brains all over his own Vietnam memorial.

Well, killer boy, I could end my letter right there, I suppose, but I don't want to. The sun's coming up. The wind is dying down and the roosters across the street are getting louder by the minute. Pilahi has two hens in her second tent and I think those old cocks know it. Keanu has the propane stove fired up, steam rising from the pot. Tea soon. The sea has a good chop on it this morning, but that doesn't mean we won't be fishing. I can feel those nets swelling with fish, but you, killer boy, you can cast your net just as far as you can throw it but you should know your net has just as many holes as it has bells and whistles. We made those holes. We know they are there. None of us fish who escaped your trap are swimming back.

Yours, Jerrycan

Low Tide

"Could you *please* watch how you are swinging that hammer?"

Marsh jerked his head around, startled to find Janie standing behind him, crowbar in hand. They had been working all summer on this derelict house, and although they'd been slaving non-stop ten hours a day, it seemed as if the job just kept growing bigger, fatter, larger, day by day by day. Today, the whole project felt like a balloon ready to burst, or perhaps one that had already burst. There was nothing inflated about this scene.

When Janie looked around, all she saw were broken bits of plaster lathe, bare wires exploding from walls, dust, dirt, broken glass, and a staircase leading nowhere. Last week, they had finally acknowledged that nothing they might do would save the second-story yellow pine floor. As beautiful as it might be, the water damage from the leaking roof was too great. Granted, the roof had been fixed – that was the first thing they did – but when they began pry up the spongy rotted floor boards, they discovered an infestation of beetles that seemed to creep upward downward and outward, which meant the joists would need to be replaced – and if the joists were to be ripped out, of course, the first floor ceiling would also necessarily disappear, and who knew if the beetle trails reached the wall studs. It seemed as if every time they went to catch a wave, they were caught in a riptide and shuttled so far from shore that it was hard to figure out just how they would paddle back. Janie couldn't understand why Marsh was nailing back the windowsill on the stairwell that had been kicked free as they dragged the last of the damaged floorboards down the stair and out to the dumpster in the driveway. It seemed rather pointless, but then again, nailing something down was at least one small possible achievement in the middle of a swelling sea of impossibility.

"Marsh," Janie breathed. "Don't you think that maybe Mako had a point? Maybe we should just hire a bulldozer, take this rattle-trap rat-trap down and start anew? See if the foundation is secure enough to support a new structure? Aren't we just pulling it down piece by piece anyway?"

Mako had come with them when they flew to Hawai`i a year ago. He had been quite the builder in his day but at 88 was now too frail to do much more than offer advice. At first, he came with them every day and sat quietly on his canvas backed fold-up chair, balanced on what remained of the porch, offering terse suggestions about how to discover which walls could be safely removed, which must stay as load-bearing walls. Janie found his advice thoughtful, reasonable, and generally useful, but Marsh had more difficulty hearing anything his father said.

Marsh stubbornly plowed ahead, and eventually Mako stopped speaking, just sat with his back to the peeling clapboards, smoking cigarette after cigarette until the day was done and it was time to pack up and go home. One morning he left his chair folded neatly behind the kitchen door. As they gathered their tools at dawn and got ready to fire up the old truck, Mako poured cup of coffee, gestured at it and the sinkful of dishes, shook his head, and clicked his tongue against the top of his mouth. He apologized, mumbling something about his back and walked them to the door, his hand resting lightly on Janie's arm. Then holding the screen door open with one hand and keeping his other hand flat against the kitchen wall, he had said quietly *you clean up that mess and I'll clean up this one.*

But what if there was no cleaning it up?

Two years ago, when the beach left suddenly, there had been plenty to clean up, but that clean-up had been predictable. This old house less so. Then, the sea was thick with lumber, square timbers still lashed together with sisal rope, boards floating free, some still draped with canvas sheeting. None of it familiar, except for the two bright green lawn chairs that floated up on the beach the afternoon of the second day. Janie recognized those as the two chairs the man in the yellow ball cap had set in front of his hastily constructed "beach house" before planting a pirate flag down by the water's edge.

Before tacking that silly sign "Om Sweet Om" behind his surfboards next to the palm tree in front of her naupaka hedge. Before all that.

The waves had arrived suddenly and were very large but not unexpected. Every year the beach came and went. Every spring the sea came up to take away the tons and tons of sand that had been deposited just as the winter swells began. During the winter the naupaka hedge ended at the dry reef gently lapped by waves. In the summer months the shoreline was across a sandy beach hundreds of feet beyond the hedge. By fall, it seemed as if the beach would always be there, but Janie knew that it would leave and that sometimes its departure would be precipitous. Others, especially those who had recently arrived on the island from steel and glass cities, had no such knowledge.

Dan was one of those others. He showed up one morning before dawn, yahooing like a drunk cowboy on a wild horse, standing stiff-legged astride one of those big-wheeled trikes that could drive anywhere, even through deep sands. Careening back and forth behind him was a trailer stacked with recycled lumber, a portable generator, and power tools. By seven a.m., his circular saw slicing through two by fours had awakened the entire neighborhood. By 7:15, Janie, always the peacemaker, was out on the beach with two cups of coffee in hand.

"Excuse me." She waited until he turned off the saw, then held out a cup of coffee and introduced herself before asking him as firmly and as quietly as possible, "What are you doing?"

Pulling a red bandana from his pocket, he swiped off his traffic yellow ball cap and mopped rivers of sweat from his neck before turning ever so slowly towards Janie. He picked up his hammer but made no move to accept the steaming coffee. "What do you think I'm doing? Ain't it obvious? I'm building."

"Listen," Janie paused, "sir, you can't . . ."

Before she could finish her sentence, he was shouting. "Don't tell me what I can or can't do, lady. I'm Dan. Dan *the Man*. You can call me Dan-o, and I will tell you I have as much right to be on this beach as you do. Yes sirree, this is public property right up to the high tide line and I am about as public as they come, so looks to me like I have as much right to be here as you do and . . ."

"Look." Janie figured it was her turn to interrupt. "You're right, Dan-o. It's a public beach but even if you are 'Dan the Man,' you really shouldn't build even a temporary shack here."

He scrunched his eyes into a thick purpled line and took one step towards her. "What, lil lady, you think my nice neat one room beach house will mess up your view? Tough."

Janie took one look at the hammer, held up both hands and stepped back.

"It's not that, really," Janie too a deep breath and tried again.

She wanted to tell him about the shifting sands, that he was building on a beach that would be gone sooner rather than later, but Dan the Man was in no mood to listen and he had all the noisemakers necessary to drown her out. When Janie opened her mouth to speak, he grabbed his power saw, held it above his head and throttled down until the sharp-edged whine bounced from the waves, cutting through the more peaceful sounds of wind whistles, dove voice, distance, and memory.

Janie figured she'd give him the benefit of the doubt. "Powerful south swell forecast for the week-end, and you know what that means."

"Do I ever! Great! Yahoo!! Go get 'em tiger!" He rolled his eyes and shrugged his shoulder in the direction of his surfboard planted upright in the sand. "I'm ready. Can't wait to get on the waves again, show father Neptune what I'm made of."

"Nothing but bones and blood," Janie muttered as he turned and kicked showers of sand backward like some old horse. Janie stepped aside. "Really, Dan, I would think again about putting so much effort into building your beach shack. The waves will eat you. The sea is as hungry as your are."

"The waves will eat me?!? Whoa, *ho*, I'm scared. The big bad monster sea is going to chew me up and swallow me down. I ain't Jonah, lady, and besides, the last I checked, whales stay off shore. You're funny, ha ha, but seriously, girlie, why don't you just leave me be and go back to trimming your hedge? I won't say a thing about your lawns, and you just keep your pretty little mouth shut about my surf shack, okay? I'm not worried about being eaten. The last I looked waves are still toothless."

Janie had wanted to say something about the difference between looking and seeing, but she knew there was no arguing with this guy. She called Marsh and he called the beach patrol but the beach patrol said they were too busy pulling tourists out of the surf to deal with some crazy who wanted to build some kind of makeshift temporary shelter. There was no convincing them that this guy was building like he meant to stay and that he was building in the washout zone.

Dan the Man finished building by nightfall, and when Marsh got home, he went down to talk to him. Janie stood in the yard and watched. By the looks of things, Marsh didn't have any more luck convincing old Dan-o that his shack – temporary or not – was definitely in danger of washing out. The next morning Dan-the-Man was still there, sitting on his bright green lawn chair, coffee cup in hand. By afternoon, he was out on the waves as the waves were busily nibbling away the beach. By evening, at the far end of the beach, the sandy slope between the seawall and the waves had disappeared beneath the breakers and what had been a beach was now a cove. All night, Janie lay awake as the volume of the waves steadily increased, but the following morning good ole Dan-o was still there, unconcerned that the shoreline had crept closer to his beach hut overnight. Marsh went again to try and convince Dan to examine soberly the evidence that the sea had provided in the past few days, but Dan had simply shrugged, grabbed his board and yelled over his shoulder as he leapt into the surf.

Not so far to walk now, man. Me and the sea, me and the sea, blood brothers, attached at the fins.

"Blood and bones," Janie whispered, "bones and blood."

Maybe it had to do with the earthquakes rocking the southern seas, but that southern swell was larger than any in recent years. The waves kept growing larger and hungrier as the night grew deeper. Dawn approached like a spider, slowly carefully, and well-disguised, but nonetheless, by morning the sea was depositing at the far end of the beach the last of the great armloads of sand sucked from other end of the beach. As the sand came ashore so did two-by-fours and plastic lawn chairs, eaten by the waves and spit out as indigestible. No bodies, of course. Dan was stubborn but not stupid. He easily escaped but never retrieved much from the ruins of his shack other than one green chair. Marsh, Mako, and the lifeguards worked overtime to clear the beach. Houses, it seems, are easier to build than to retrieve.

Or resurrect. Janie set her crowbar down and watched as Marsh continued to nail the wayward windowsill into place.

"Marsh." Janie unbuttoned the top two buttons of her shirt and then buttoned them up again. "Marsh, does that sill really matter? What are we doing here, Marsh, what are we doing?"

Marsh gave the nail one more tap and looked up. With his back to her, he gestured toward the sea, moving his arm in a wide circle before dropping it at his side. When he turned to look at her, he was smiling.

Victory Gardens

When Shane planted the New Zealand spinach seed he had gathered at the beach some months before, he knew he was planting a weed but he wanted a vegetable that would grow easily in the salt spray, a green he could harvest at any time of the year, substantial and hearty enough to eat as a main course alongside his rice. At home on rocky seacoasts, New Zealand spinach, with its thick leaves and spreading habit, seemed a natural as fresh available food at all times of the year. It grew as a ground cover at the very edge of the bay, one plant stretching to cover ten or twelve feet of dry sand. The birds loved it; small critters loved it, burrowing deep beneath its shallow roots and popping up amongst its dense tangled foliage, but he also knew it could as easily overwhelm his small but more orderly garden space. It was definitely weedy, not nearly as tasty as "real" spinach, but he planted it anyway.

Lately he had been living within some dark cloud of foreboding, feeling a bit like one of those cartoon doomsayers, dressed in white robes and standing on a bustling street corner holding a battered hand-written sign *The End is Near*. Obviously, if the end was near, it was the end of that emaciated character with the matted hair, not the world. Now, here he was, planting "survival" gardens, his own version of the *End is Near* sign. Silly really.

He had spent countless hours arguing with himself about just how silly it was, but he couldn't shake the feeling. So, he kept on planting, reminding himself that "silly" was a word that derived from the Old English word for blessed, *saelig*. To be silly was to look for beauty, maybe even to pray, to be blessed. Silliness as prayer. He could live with that. Of course, planting gardens in response to some illogical sneaking suspicion of impending doom made no sense. If the earth's crust buckled and a tsunami traveled at speed across the sea, if icebergs melted and caused the oceans to swell past the limits of their banks, if Haleakala decided to suddenly slide into the sea, everything would be swept away, including the house, including him, including her. But watching things grow made all the sense in the world.

His sister had called him months and months ago and asked if she might visit. Of course, he had said yes. It had been years, and he had so much to show her, including this handmade house blooming from the foundation of the house where they had lived as kids. He wanted to tell her how he had carefully dismantled the old house, stacking the massive beams to use as framing timbers, tossing out the pine paneling riddled with insect holes, saving the koa flooring. He'd show her how the old windows had finally found new life high on the kitchen wall where their thick wavy glass might twist and turn the last of the afternoon light. He wanted her to enjoy that late light while sitting on the stone terrace he had built facing the sea. They'd watch the sun slip into the sea and he'd explain how he had hauled tons of lava rock and slabs of ancient coral from the old abandoned ruin down the road, how he had spent months sorting the stones, setting aside as terrace stones the ones with broad flat faces, stacking the rounder stones as border walls. He wanted her to see herself in this new house, drink tea sitting on the bench he had built in the inner courtyard beneath the breadfruit tree she had planted on her ninth birthday. He wanted her to know her tree was no longer outside struggling against the valley winds, to show her how its thick branches, heavy with fruit, balanced above the delicate forest ferns he had planted below. He wanted her to feel as he did, to know that by protecting her tree from the wind, by making sure it had light and rain, he was protecting her. He'd wanted a lot in those days.

He spent the week prior to her scheduled arrival recreating as private space the screen porch with its wide sea views and climbing lilikoi vines. He moved in a bed with a comfortable mattress, positioned a wicker chair near the window closest to the waves, hemmed delicate lace curtains and threaded them over bamboo rods. The day of the flight he rubbed almond oil onto the new counters, washed the floors with coconut oil soap, and made sure every room had fresh flowers in blue glass vases. No roses, but flowers from the mountain – white ginger, red ginger, plumerias floating in shallow crystal bowls.

Shane knew how much Lizzie loved flowers. Even when she lived in wilds of South Brooklyn, she had planted a hedge of climbing roses that bloomed extravagantly every spring. Liz had moved to Brooklyn when rents in Manhattan went sky high. Artists can't pay high rents and still make art. She found first a loft on the waterfront and then, when the neighborhood was 'discovered' and the rents began to climb, moved to a falling down house further south, deeper into the ghetto. She called him, after moving, sick with worry about the kids and the daily gunfire, unsure what to do about the fenceless backyard.

No barbed wire, she printed on the back of a post card of the Statue of Liberty. She hated chain-link fences, hated razor wire, barbed wire, all the scabby protective devices of the ghetto, but the vision of incoherent junkies wandering into the backyard while her baby son was pushing his bright yellow dump trucks through the dirt terrified her. She lay awake at night worrying. She called to tell him about a picture she had found in a catalog of some obscure nursery in the Midwest – a hedge of Robin Hood Roses so pink, so lush that it reminded her of the luscious pudding their mother used to make after spending the afternoon gathering strawberry guava up on Tantalus. Nothing was ever so pink. Made her mouth water just looking at the picture. She decided. No fence. Just roses. *Robin Hood, Shane, Robin Hood.* She laughed so hard he had to laugh too even though he wasn't sure why. *Robin Hood Roses. Six bushes for six dollars. Roses, Shane! Roses!*

He wasn't surprised that when the bushes came, she called again. Nobody sells six bushes of anything for six dollars, even then. She was beside herself. He had to hold the phone inches from his ear. *These aren't bushes! They're twigs smaller than my smallest finger, Shane, twigs with hair roots! Twigs! If they live, they'll take decades to grow, Shane, decades!*

She planted them anyway, dug tiny little holes, buried the tiny little twigs in those tiny little holes and marked each burial with a chopstick. To her surprise (and his), they grew – and grew and

GREW. More like Jack and his Magic Beans than Robin Hood and his Merry Men. Within two months, the border between her yard and the next was overwhelmed by thorny canes covered in apple green leaves. After three months, there were flowers, surprising bouquets of diminutive pink roses with a delicate perfume that fanned away all leftover fumes from idling trucks. Within four months, every room in her falling down house overflowed with armloads of roses, spilling from blue glass vases.

He had thought about buying cut roses, but Lizzie was not one for hothouse flowers and he knew no one who grew roses on this side of the island and even if they did, he was fairly sure they wouldn't measure up to the weedy wild roses of Liz's long ago hedge. The night of the plane, he had waited with a pikake lei, his back pressed against the pillar, watching as dozens of travelers, bleary-eyed after their nine-hour flight stumbled over to the baggage belt, heaved overloaded suitcases into carts and left. He waited until the crowd had thinned to ten and then to one. He couldn't imagine Liz as the sharp-faced bone-thin woman standing with her back to the far wall, staring as the glass doors slid open then shut, open then shut, but when he approached, she turned.

Hello, Shane. Something flashed then closed.

They drove the long road home, mountains on their left, swelling waves on the right and he chattered nonstop, telling her this and that about the house, describing his fledgling vegetable garden, the surf, last night's moon. He kept talking after parking the car in the carport, after carrying her suitcases into her newly painted room, and she never said a word.

As he prepared the tea and put the scones baked that morning onto copper-glazed plates, he told her the story of the pigs on the beach after the great rainstorm, described the ten waterfalls on the mountain face that sparkled like ice. He filled her in on the most recent political brouhahas, laughing at the absurdity of it, bemoaning the seriousness of it. He explained about the hot water heater and the banging pipe (he was working on it), told her where the tea was kept. When he asked her which mug she wanted for her tea, he wasn't surprised when she picked the one with roses. When he asked where she wanted to keep her toothbrush in the bathroom, on the bottom shelf or the top, he was surprised when she didn't answer. When he asked again, she moved her hand from her face and let her fingers fan across the tablecloth until her thumb brushed the sugar dish. She smiled. At least he thought she smiled. She didn't speak, and hasn't spoken to him or anyone since *Hello, Shane.*

At first, her silence was like a sharp blade scraping every surface in the house. The counters dulled. Window panes massed with scratches so dense that light refused to enter, but as weeks passed, as weeks turned into months, the high pitched whine of silence scraping stone settled into a balanced bass and treble with a comfortable rhythm of its own.

Now, he needs to plant weeds.

Coda

Karin paused, let her thumb jostle the far edge of the orchid, and then stood back and watched as the flower bobbed and fluttered like some exotic butterfly from a country where she had never been. The large purple flower with its trembling petals and damp lips was the only one like it in the store, and Karin was sure that her auntie would love to see such a flower balanced on the narrow collapsible table near her hospital bed, the only piece of furniture in the room other than the stiff green vinyl chair where Karin perched when she came to visit. The flower was perfect, but when she turned over the price tag, she gasped.

Seventy-eight dollars for one flower attached to one stem with two broad leather-like leaves. Why it didn't even seem like the poor plant had any dirt. The roots looked like so many dried worms trying desperately to escape the confines of the tiny black plastic pot tucked not-so-neatly into a cheap wicker basket. $78!

Karin turned to examine the rows of potted tulips near the window, each pot tied with a brightly colored ribbon, but as she turned, the great purple flower gasped and breathed. A delicate aroma – a pale wind – brushed her cheek, and suddenly she felt intoxicated. How could a flower do that? She was convinced that when she had had her face near the crinkled mouth of the orchid, she had smelled nothing, but this thin spicy almost blue scent that landed on her cheek could have only come from the orchid. She edged closer to the tulips, put her face near their waxy buds and breathed. Nothing but the scent of damp earth, reminding of Uncle Arthur's farm upstate. Aunt Martha might like to be reminded of her kitchen garden coming to life in the spring.

She picked up a pot of yellow tulips, inches from bloom, carried them to the cashier, but just as she set the pot down, the orchid sighed and its perfumed breath tangled delicately and discretely with the sturdy tulip buds. The sales clerk reached behind her for scissors to cut the tag from the tulips, and as she did, Karin yanked the pot towards her.

"Wait. I need to ask you something."

The salesgirl removed her glasses, wiped them carefully with her bright pink apron. "Okay, but ya gotta know, I only help out here on Sundays. Don't know much about the care and feeding of plants."

"That's okay. It's not that." Karin tapped her fingers on the counter lightly as if recalling a difficult piano arpeggio. "I was just thinking, if you were recovering from a mastectomy, would you rather have spring flowers that remind you of wonderful days in the past spent at home or something, well, different, something exotic, something new?"

She bent backwards, leaning towards the orchid, hoping the girl might notice the magnetism between her and the flower, but girl simply looked puzzled. She couldn't have been more than fifteen years old. When she smiled her braces caught the light, but the smile was forced, the gapped grin of someone either uncomfortable or bored. Or both.

"A Mass-tech-toe-Me." She rolled the word forward to the front of her mouth before pushing it past her braces. "What's that?"

Now, it was Karin's turn to be uncomfortable. How was she going to explain to this young teenager about breast cancer, how the cutting away of cancerous flesh sometimes meant that a breast must be removed, leaving a woman with scarred skin stretched over ribs?

"Do you mind if I sit down for a moment?"

Karin gestured towards the faux Victorian parlor chairs tucked between the two glass-fronted display cases, overwhelmed by bouquets of roses, baby's breath, and peonies stilled tightly closed.

The sales girl shrugged. "Suit yourself. I don't have any place to go. Yet." She glanced knowingly at her watch.

It was not that Karin couldn't explain. After all she was a doctor, quite used to explaining trauma to the young women who sat every day in her office sputtering out confused questions with their hands trapped beneath thighs, eyes brimming, lips trembling. She had this speech down pat, starting slow, patiently enunciating every word, and never ever forgetting to smile brightly just before the chirpy lines about reconstructive surgery. It wasn't that she couldn't explain or that she didn't felt a responsibility to explain, she did, but she didn't want to. This was her Aunt Martha.

Explain now and she would be back at the lake with her cousin Jenny, racing down the hill throwing clothing onto blueberry bushes, plowing full speed into cold water. How their skin puckered and blued until they seemed as rocky as the drying streamed in August. On the days Uncle Arthur and Aunt Martha came down to swim, they too ran headlong down hill, and when Martha threw off her wide skirt, she whipped it three times about her head before releasing it to the uphill winds, hoping it would catch a particularly strong breeze and blossom like a rose. One afternoon, just as thunderheads were gathering, all that fabric caught a ride on a strong gust and landed in the highest branches of the apple tree. They all collapsed laughing in the tall grass, Martha's generous breasts bobbing up and down as she laughed, reminding Karin she too might one day be the caretaker of such beauty. Later that evening, Arthur fetched the ladder and carefully pulled the pink cloth from the gnarled apple branches, tied it around his waist and filled it with all the ripe apples within reach. After supper, he presented the neatly folded skirt to Martha with a late summer rose laid on top. *You are my rose* he had said and she'd smiled. Karin would swear in court that her smile lit up that corner of the room. She and Jenny took apples to bed that night.

Now, she just didn't feel like outlining the clinical details of cancer treatment to this young woman lounging behind the counter. It was too complicated. Years ago when her grandfather was dying of liver cancer, she had come face-to-face with death for the first time and had been surprised. She'd always assumed that when death came, one simply succumbed, and that was it. The trick, she thought, to facing death was to accept it and thus go peacefully and hopefully painlessly. But Grandpa had refused. Choosing life at all costs, he lay in that narrow hospital bed for months, growing thinner and thinner until his skin was like oiled parchment stretched ever so delicately over brittle bones. Time after time, she received frantic calls from her mother telling her to come now, the doctors were announcing that death was near, and time after time, she leapt on a plane, flew home, hurried to the hospital only to find Grandpa demanding more pillows and a stronger light so he could read. Seeing her, he'd rasp *so they sent for you again . . . I tell you, K, I'm not going anywhere until I finish reading these books,* and then he'd mumble something about nobody ever listening to him. Ever.

She'd laugh and he'd give her one of those crooked lopsided smiles he had at the end.

Her grandfather had decided half way through his first go with chemotherapy that he really didn't know enough about the Pacific and that he knew next to nothing about the history of the Hawaiian Islands, bits of land he loved with more passion than seemed reasonable to Karin who had been born and bred in New England. He begged Karin to find him books to read, and she had scoured the city library shelves, borrowing rather than buying, thinking this a very temporary passion. When, at her grandfather's request, she found herself renewing again and again the books, she gave up and ordered books from any number of booksellers to be sent posthaste to the hospital, which made her grandfather happy. Having ownership of the books, he could scribble as many notes as he wanted in the margins. How, he said, would he remember what he needed to know without those notes?

She was mystified by his need to remember when he knew he was dying, but she didn't raise an eyebrow as he assiduously transferred onto the pages of his new books the contents of the tiny notebooks he had been using while still carefully handling the library books. He painstakingly read all of David Malo, John Papa I'i, Martha Beckwith, everything that Mary Kawena Pukui had written or edited. He wrote letters to living writers who shared with him new titles, sent articles and unpublished essays. He read and read, and just when she thought he had read everything that had ever been written about Hawai'i, he handed her a new list of out-of-print books. Hard to find, but she managed.

She had done her best, spending days sifting through titles at the Strand and hours in conversation with booksellers in London and New Zealand. One thing she knew for sure -- if there was anyone who took more seriously than her grandfather that old saw about death being a beginning not an ending, she didn't know who that might be. Eventually, he told her emphatically that she really shouldn't bother flying in when the doctors announced his death as imminent. *He,* he said, would give her plenty of advance notice, and he did.

Shortly after she graduated Med school and became Dr. Karin Thorsen, he called while she was doing rounds, left a message with her answering service. *Karin, I'm on the second volume of* Nana i ke Kumu. *It's the last book, Karin. I'll be finished by Wednesday.*

Finished. His words. His work would be done. The message came on a Friday; she swallowed once, fought back tears. Then, she gathered herself together and went to speak with those who needed to know, booked a flight arriving in Boston Tuesday morning.

When she walked into the hospital room, she was sure he looked thinner and more worn. His skin was insecurely yellow, but there was nothing vague about his eyes, nothing tentative about his smile. She could tell he was tired but also oddly that he had decided. This was it. No question. He gestured his welcome, waved her to sit close to the bed. His gestures although brief were as definite as those of a conductor. There could be no question as to who was leading this orchestra. She listened to his thoughts about *Nana i ke Kumu.* He begged her to read the book as they sat together quietly before her mother arrived, then her father, her aunt, her uncle, her cousin, his brother, his cousin. Only after they had all crowded into the room, only after he had made sure all players in his personal orchestra were present and accounted for, only then did he smile gently, whisper two words *thank you* and close his eyes. He took a breath so long so deep that she thought he would swallow the world.

Maybe he did.

At first she had been bemused by his desire to read throughout those long months of chemotherapy and then to continue reading when the doctors told him cancer had signed his death warrant, that there would be no surviving this. Nothing in her medical textbooks had mentioned reading as an expected response to a diagnosis of "no survival possible." Somehow she found it easier to accept those who decided they wanted to travel or eat foods never tasted, listen to soothing music or to watch musicals over and over again. She understood those who wanted to close their eyes and have someone read *to* them – romance novels, mysteries, chirpy cheerful stories about staying *strong* – but she was mystified by her grandfather's choice. Why would anyone want to read *history* at the end, but here was her own grandfather insisting that he would not go to his grave without knowing the history of a place he loved but did not understand. Reading history, especially history that demanded an understanding of a culture quite foreign to him, was strenuous yet he read and read and read – until he was finished reading. Maybe, she thought, that's what we do, read our world.

"Hey." Karin looked up. The sales girl was leaning with her elbows on the counter, her head resting on her cupped hands.

"Hey, you okay? I'd let you sit there all night but I gotta close." This time she didn't glance at her watch but tapped it emphatically. "I can't leave someone sitting like a statue in the window. You wanna buy something or not?"

"Oh, yes." Karin stood, smoothed her skirt, and smiled. "Sorry."
She turned and picked up the purple orchid just as it breathed, releasing again its fine net of deep perfume.

"I'll take this. New information, I think, is more important than old. Gotta keep reading."

When she stepped outside, a light snow was beginning to fall, and Karin was glad for the extra layers of cellophane the salesclerk had insisted on piling over the orchid.

Only eight blocks to walk.

ua pau ka pilikia, ua hala ka `ino, ua kau ka mālie
e ho`omaha kākou me ka maluhia
a me ke aloha nui loa

mahalo ia kākou

∞

Tia Ballantine is a writer and a painter, born in Peru, who has lived here there and everywhere but has most recently moved to the desert near the Mexican border. Her poems have been published in various journals, including: *Mixed Nerve; Spillway; Saw Palm; Snakeskin Webzine; Queer Poetry; War, Literature and the Arts; Hawai`i Pacific Review; Poets Canvas; Five Fingers Review; The Red Wheelbarrow; Pirene's Fountain Poetry Review; HIart*, and *The Midwest Quarterly: A Journal of Contemporary Thought.* Her work has been anthologized in Sam Hamill's *Poets Against the War* and in *Winter Gifts,* published in Scotland by Happenstance Press. She has also published short stories, essays and poetry reviews.

E lele pono, e maliu mai i ka leo o ke ola.

*****

Made in the USA
San Bernardino, CA
20 July 2017